The Panda Chronicles

Published in the United States by
Five Birds Publishing
603-G Avenida Sevilla
Laguna Woods, CA 92637

The characters and events in this book are fictitious. Any similarity to real persons, living or dead, is coincidental and not intended by the author.

Printed in the United States of America on acid-free paper.

2015
Second Printing

The Panda Chronicles

Gordon Richiusa

Dedication by Rico Rose

My contribution to this book is that I was an undercover police officer known as The Panda, on the streets. My dedication is to my family. Thank you Gordon Richiusa for giving some of my stories a more permanent and interesting form.

Author's Acknowledgement

A special thanks to Detective Tim Kohl for previewing the original manuscript and keeping me honest and realistic in my depiction of a profession that I have the greatest respect for, protecting and serving all people, around the world.

--GFR

Cover Design by Gordon Richiusa
Cover Art by Austin Boyd

Introduction
By
Admiral, Frank W. Dux, KY.

Just like the title character in this novel, the *real life* Panda is a stocky, Hispanic, Jewish, Sherlock Holmes...an honest to goodness novelty, whose true story is stranger than fiction and probably can't be fully told to civilians who might find it incredulous since they have no frame of reference. That is, in addition to the fact it can't be told in order to protect the innocent, ongoing operations, and the tactics being employed. However, that does not diminish the fact this work is *based in truth*.

Being personally knowledgeable of the real life "Panda" (undercover officer Rico Rose) and his real life exploits I must emphasize, THIS IS A FICTION NOVEL!

Confusion may be attributable to the fact the book's author Gordon Richiusa is both a journalist (presenting only the facts) and a fiction writer (where he emphasizes telling a good story and has to make up situations and people to fit the storyline). As Ian Fleming, the creator of the James Bond franchise based his characters on real people and incidents from his days as Deputy Director of Her Majesty's Secret Service MI5, during World War II, so Gordon Richuisa relies on personal experience to salt his tales, as any good writer might do.

For instance, in his work *Shidoshi: The Four Ways of the Corpse,* author Gordon Richuisa implanted a character that resembled me in this work of fiction and because it dealt with a conflict between ninja practitioners in the U.S. and around the world--which was actually occurring in real life--people assume that the characters are totally real as well as the incidents. The reality is that *Shidoshi,* like *The Panda Chronicles* is where fact meets fiction, and that is what good *fiction* writers do. They write about things that they know and Gordon Richiusa—who is both a martial artist and worked with cops for more than two decades--is no different than Ian Fleming, Tom Clancy, etc.

Since the story, characters and events ring so true in this fictional work it is easy to forget this is a work of *fiction.* Especially, when you consider it is formulated by the author having combined two previously separate works; originally, the first half, with slight variation, was written by Gordon as, *Death Of The Panda,* which outlines Rico's years as an undercover police officer for the City of San Fernando in the Los Angeles area.

The original title of that book is based upon the fact that Rico's official police career was cut short by five gunshot wounds he received during a drug bust in 1978. It marked a death of *innocence* and political naiveté of an undercover narcotics officer.

Rico was thought to be dead and many of those who had gone to jail because of Rico's efforts had "crossed out his name," as gang members and underworld figures do, to indicate that The Panda was no more. Rico did not die as expected and the manuscript that Gordon wrote for Rico, *The Death of the Panda* was read into the public record as testimony for litigation brought to secure benefits for The Panda's retirement. This book is *not* that story, but notwithstanding it is based upon a *real life person* who is one of my past associates who served as an intelligence asset - Rico Rose.

Outside of myself, there is no other undercover investigator like Rico Rose whose reputation preceded him, as having the capability to discern the truth from a minimal amount of information, the kind you'd expect from a Sherlock Holmes novel. His skill is of the kind that at times is so razor sharp and precise that the apprehended criminals confided they called it frightening. He was *the perfect investigator* and perhaps that is why Rico found himself one day walking a political tightrope, why he was shot five times in the leg by a fellow officer during what should have been a routine drug bust. We'll never know and these unusual circumstances culminated in his meeting and inspiring Gordon Richiusa to write this novel.

With a leading character being based loosely upon me in another work by Gordon Richiusa, it was most appropriate that Rico Rose wrote the introduction to that novel which is entitled, *Shidoshi: The Four Ways of the Corpse.* Likewise, I was more than pleased when asked by Gordon Richiusa to introduce this fictional story based upon Rico Rose. After all, I personally relied upon Rico's services in the past, a covert operative.

To end any confusion or speculation I emphasize that like the John Suess character loosely based upon me in Shidoshi:The Four Ways of the Corpse, this is a work of fiction--thought provoking entertainment whose protagonist The Panda is based upon a real person. Any resemblance to actual persons living or dead (other than Rico Rose himself) is purely coincidental. However, when cops read this, they will see the truth in the characters, situations and words.

If you seek investigative journalism, I invite you to read Gordon's and my column, *Legends and Legacies* at WorldWideDojo.com. You wont be disappointed as we ask the difficult questions of Living Legends. We do so in order to provide an objective platform for them to candidly speak for themselves, unedited and without commentary. In doing so, we dare sort out and expose truth from media hype and spin, with their failing to present the whole truth, often due to misconceptions and broadcast time constraints.

Rico Rose is very concerned that people do not make the same mistake with his story as they did with *Bloodsport*, a movie that was made about my life, that starred and launched the film career of Jean Claude Van Damme; having resulted in people sometimes going so far as confusing the actor and myself as one in the same person.

In as much as Rico Rose is a real person, a real detective called The Panda on the mean streets of Los Angeles barrios, he will be glad to tell you which parts of this story are true and which are not. But, whenever justice might be compromised by Rico revealing certain facts...well, he wisely keeps those facts to himself. In real life he may start a story with, *"Well, I can't tell you everything..."*

Today, Rico is a private-citizen whose real-life adventures are confined to his story telling. His children think he is a great teddy bear of a dad, and have no connection to his past. With them he begins every tale, tongue in cheek--and you have to grin as he whispers gently to them, *"There I was, in the face of danger..."*

Chapter One
Good Dies Hard

The homemade blade, fashioned to look like a small Samurai sword seemed to imitate the setting sun, thrusting deep into the slain man as the last ray of sunlight glistened on the blade as it entered the flesh of the man's body like the sunset dropping over the horizon. The man being killed almost admired the craftsmanship of the polished blade that caught the fading sunlight, accenting the artistry of his killer. The killer was the man they called *Paloma*. The knife slashed, cut, and stabbed the victim countless times, but not a single drop of blood fell before the victim, a seemingly insignificant man in a blue beanie collapsed to the asphalt.

"It can't end like this," The man thought to himself as he lay limp and dying, face down on the dirty street. It all had happened too fast. One moment, he was talking to Paloma and the next he was dead. The mini Passion Play had been performed on a suburban street in the heart of the San Fernando Valley.

It was like a scene from an old Western movie. The two must have appeared to one another like gunfighters on an old western street, first just specks, growing larger, the closer he'd gotten.

He had seen Paloma, from afar as a man alone, walking restlessly back and forth on the sidewalk. Paloma looked to one end of the horizon, turned, and walked back a few paces gazing in the direction from which he'd come. He imagined how Paloma must have perceived him, as well. The wind had stopped in that frozen time between daylight and evening and there were no sounds except for those of some far away traffic and the shuffling of his and Paloma's feet along the sidewalk.

After several seconds of this pacing, Paloma who was dressed in a T-shirt, khaki Levis and a red, bandana, seemed to see his soon-to-be victim in the distance and relaxed. The second man was dressed similarly, but he wore no bandana, but a blue beanie. The two men did not know one another, but there was no one else around, so Paloma must have assumed that this man had come here specifically to find him. That was an essential part of his business, *being found.* There was no reason for anyone else to be walking on this desolate street as he saw the other man rising up from the horizon. Paloma knew that one of his associates must have sent this man to him.

Earlier, the man in the blue beanie had been on a treasure hunt to find Paloma. He had met an intermediary, known as *Stranger* on a nearby street. The earlier meeting had gone like this:

"Horale, Carnal!" The man in the blue beanie had started the conversation. They had stood on the same corner together for several minutes, saying nothing to one another. These words were the first outward sign that the men had any interest in each other.

"Stranger, I need a fix. I'm hurting," the one wearing the beanie rubbed both arms with the palms of his hands simultaneously, as if he were cold on this hot summer evening.

After an evil smile, Stranger said, "You know I'm not a dealer, man. But, if you turn me on to a five, I'll point you in the right direction."

The man in the beanie thought a moment, shrugged his shoulders and reached into his shoe for a five-dollar bill. Stranger took the money, not looking at it and swiftly slid it into his pocket, almost as if no money was ever mentioned.

"*Mi Carnal*, Paloma, is a good man and can do you *firme*. I happen to know that if you go to the corner of West and Ninth, you will find him sitting in the shade there."

"How will I know him?"

"*Es un vato loco*." Stranger laughed as if he's just made a hilarious joke. "He's tall and thin and wearing a blue shirt and red bandana like mine."

"*Gracias, mi carnal. Muchas gracias*." The man in the beanie was already moving away at a hurried pace, before finishing his statement. This would have been expected behavior from a junkie who was looking to score.

Stranger watched the man in the beanie for a few seconds, then his expressionless face gained a peculiar smile. The smile slowly dissolved and he spit on the sidewalk where the other man had been standing. Stranger exited the area in the opposite direction.

A few minutes later, as the sun has just set, the man in the beanie walked past a street sign on a corner. It designated that he was at the intersection of West and Ninth. There was a steady drone of cars on a nearby freeway that overpowered the scene but faded to the background. As the man was walking he was also looking. He noticed Paloma, the man he is looking for sitting under a tree near the wall of a building. There was a large amount of graffiti on the wall, mostly in Spanish or in a language that was known only to those who wrote on walls. The man in the beanie walked directly up to Paloma, who did not look up.

"They call me *Sleepy*. Stranger sent me." Sleepy got right to the point.

Turning his head casually and smiling, Paloma responded, "If you are an amigo of Stranger's you are firme. What are you using?"

"*Chivas*. I need it badly. Stranger told me that you are the main man here."

As if immune to the obvious butt-kissing, Paloma responded coldly with a direct question, "How much?"

"A spoon."

Paloma reached around, behind the tree and grabbed a handful of grass from the tiny patch that surrounded trunk. He wiggled the sod a few times and a small, square section lifted up. Underneath the sod were six or seven tiny balloons. These were filled with heroin. Paloma took one of the balloons, replaced the grass and stood up. With his heel he tapped the sod into place, stuffed the balloon into his pocket and began to walk.

Sleepy was a little surprised and asked, "What's wrong?"

Stopping to respond, "I don't like to deal in the open," Paloma snapped and began walking again.

The two men walked around the back of the nearest house and into an alley.

When they were tucked neatly from plain view Paloma stopped abruptly, turned and faced the other man.

"You have the money?" Handing the balloon, the other man quickly responded by reaching again into his shoe and pulling out a single, twenty-dollar bill. Paloma exhaled with disgust as he took the twenty angrily. "You know the price is a quarter!"

In pleading tone, the one called Sleepy responded quickly, "But I had to give Stranger a five just to find you. I only have the twenty now, *ala brava.*"

Paloma simply stared coldly and Sleepy seemed to crumble emotionally under his gaze. Finally, Sleepy reached down for the additional five. While Sleepy was bending forward and both of his hands were busy, Paloma grabbed him in a headlock.

Swiftly Paloma pulled the knife that he'd just used to cut the grass and began to stab the other man repeatedly. There was a brief struggle as Sleepy attempted to reach into his belt for a gun. He was killed before he could defend himself, however as every cut and stab had landed with surgical precision, each cutting a major artery or landing on an exact location. With blood starting to stain the victim's skin and clothing, one stab to the arm and a following blow to the hand that was trying to reach for the gun. Finally, Paloma cut several of the other man's vital organs and rendered him helpless within a matter of seconds, all while controlling Sleepy with one arm.

Sleepy was released and his limp body was allowed to fall, face first to the concrete. Paloma stood over the body, emotionless for a few seconds, then reached down and took the balloon and five dollars that Sleepy still clutched in his hand. At the same time Paloma wiped the blade of his knife on the shirt of the dead man's body and smiled. He stood while smiling, then his faced slowly changed to anger and he spit, directly on the body before he departed. The swiftly moving darkness overtook the scene of the one they called Sleepy, lying in a puddle of his own blood which had just begun to pool.

A short time later, as the sun began to peek over the horizon, a police car was parked in the parking lot of a donut shop. One officer was in the car and another was just entering through the passenger's open door. In this officer's hands were two cups of coffee. The officer behind the wheel was Bill (Irish) McCoy, a big, burly looking Irishman. His partner was John Polonowski, known alternatively as Officer Big John and Rainbow Polonowski. John, also large and mean looking, had the added attribute of a pair of "cannon barrel" biceps, hence the "Big" moniker. He also joked that even though his last name was Polonowski, he has every kind of ethnicity there is running through his veins.

These two "macho" types were not well prepared for the emotional action that followed, as the car left the curb and drove into the street.

Irish said, "Where to now, bro?"

"I'm tired. Turn off at West. I always like to spin through the alleys and check what kind of garbage has been left out from the night before," said Polonowski. Both laughed.

While searching with his eyes, Irish commented, "It looks like it was a quiet night."

"Too hot for the bad guys."

"Yeah, I bet the whores couldn't get close enough to anyone to make an indecent living." Both laughed again, perhaps a little too loudly and Polonowski yawned while asking, "Is it Miller Time, yet?"

"About an hour more. Don't worry, you'll make it."

Spotting something, but not overly concerned Polonowski responded, "Looks like that one couldn't even make it home, or even out of the gutter." As the car comes to a stop he added, "This guy's right in the middle of the goddamn alley."

The two men looked at each other, disgusted.

"We've got to at least move him." Irish saw no way around the body.

"I could just back up, drive away like nothing ever happened."

"Naw. We've got to move him and you know what they say. *If you touch it, you own it.* Do you want me to call it in?"

"Not really. I'll do it," Picking up the microphone from the car radio John added, "If we don't report it, some rare, law abiding citizen is sure to drive by and report *us*."

Irish got out of car while John called on the car radio, "Twenty-five Adam seven, Station?"

A woman's voice on the car radio broke through a short burst of static. "Go ahead Twenty-five Adam seven."

"We'll be code six on a man down in the alley to the rear of West at Ninth." Officer John put back the microphone and got out of the car. As he walked over around to the body, Irish has already exited and was standing at the front of the car.

"What is it, a drunk or a hype?"

"I don't know. He used to be one of those, but now all he is, is dead."

Officer John pressed his fingers to the neck of the victim then, in a cursory search seemed to notice something, "Shit! I hate it when this happens. There's blood. Why couldn't we just have left him here? I hate putting in overtime on this crap." He walked casually back to the car as Irish casually knelt and began to search the body.

From the car, Irish heard his partner, "Twenty-five Adam seven, requesting homicide; we've got a one-eighty-seven."

"Roger. Homicide will be responding. Preserve the area."

Irish, while searching the body, finds the man's wallet and pulls it out. Flipping it open, reveals a badge on the inside. Irish's eyes widen to a look of terror and grief. As John finishes his communication on the microphone, he stands and readies to return to his partner's side. Irish is advancing towards him with the wallet and his own mouth hanging open.

Not yet noticing what Irish is carrying, John asks, "What's wrong with y...?" Then he sees the badge. "Oh, my god!"

"This dude's a cop!" He shakes his head unbelieving.

Officer John Polonowski returned to the microphone inside the car, much more animated now. "Twenty-five Adam, Station, switch to tack two," he nearly shouted in a commanding tone.

"I'm sorry. Tack two is being used." The dispatcher's voice came back quickly, appearing a little disturbed by the officer's tone.

"Damn it. Switch to tack two, right now!"

There is more static.

In an angry voice the dispatcher returns, "Fine. Tack two. What the hell's the matter with you?"

"This guy's a cop."

There was a short silence and then, as if not hearing "Go again?"

Irish was standing with the wallet and badge held at arm's length, as if what he has is the most horrible and foul thing imaginable. Officer

Big John's voice was frantic, almost crying, "Damn it! The DB! I said this guy's a cop. He's one of us! Do you understand?"

The radio immediately went static again. Within seconds the sound of sirens in the distance could be heard getting closer. There was silent grief in the countenance of the two street cops. Officer "Irish" McCoy turned away from his partner and leaned against the hood of the car. Suddenly, as if boiling to a rage, he pounded his fist into the vehicle. The hood was deeply dented and the single sound of the impact faded immediately behind the approaching sirens, after the blow was struck.

It is 7:55 a.m.

Chapter Two
Building Character and the Fifteen Minute Mystery

The day of the murder: 10:55 a.m.

Two bulky fists pound a heavy bag in a martial arts studio. The fists are attached to two, muscular arms and the short, stocky Mexican body of Rico Rose. He has a round face, large dark eyes and a mustache, which outlines his mouth. His street-name is *The Panda* and he looks remarkably like his label.

A youngster watches him from just outside, through a doorway near a sitting area inside the Isshin Ryu dojo where Rico works-out and assists with the teaching. A brown belt around Rico's waist shows that he has yet to complete his training and fully test his skills, but that he has a certain level of knowledge that deserves respect.

Rico stops punching the bag and looks at the youngster who is a small, dark-haired Latino of about 15 years of age. There are a third and fourth person further back in the studio as well. One wears a black belt.

The other instructor, wearing the black belt, clears his throat loudly to get his student's attention away from watching Rico. This is John Angel, Rico's instructor and best "non cop" friend.

John is giving another young student a lesson but the youngster isn't paying much attention. Angel is slight of build, wiry, with glasses. As he clears his throat he gets the youngster to look back, as Rico looks over to the door, stops pounding the heavy bag and goes to greet the incoming visitor.

"Excuse me sir, my name is George."

"Que paso?" Rico smiles and reaches out a hand to shake. "I'm Rico Rose. How can I help you?"

Lowering his eyes, with slight embarrassment the boy responds, "I'm interested in…I was wondering about classes."

Rico senses something is being unsaid. "Have you ever trained before?"

"Just messing around. You know. I've got friends who've studied, but I want to learn more than they can teach me."

Rico reaches for a pile of schedules that are stacked on a table in the entryway. "Every little bit helps, as long as it's in the right direction. Whatever you've learned so far is O.K. but it's good you realize that you need a qualified teacher. That shows character. Classes are every night except Sunday. These morning classes are private instructions. Sometimes a brown belt will help with teaching." Rico points down to his own belt casually, then adds, "Here's a list of what we do here, and when." He hands the boy the list. "The prices for instruction are on there."

George's face sags, sadly shocked as he glances at the brochure. "Oh? Well, thanks for your time. I'm not really sure about my schedule right now." George turns to walk away.

Rico calls the boy back with a question, before he can escape. "Do you have a job?"

Curious, George responds, "Part time. I deliver papers." He punctuates his words with a shrug.

"Could you do some work around here to pay for lessons?"

George just looks at Rico, confused by his last question. "I mean if you can work it into your schedule, especially around going to school," Rico adds. "We have a policy that you do well in school or you can't take classes…But, right now we're looking for someone to come in and clean up around here, sweep, that sort of thing."

George's face lights up. "Does the job pay anything?"

Caught off guard, Rico recovers, "Well...a...No, just lessons for work." Rico looks over and sees John has finished with his lesson and is coming over, listening to the conversation. "You know, just a trade."

George ponders only a moment then responds, "O.K. Sounds good. I mean, that's fair."

"Can you start tomorrow?"

George smiles broadly, nods his head affirmatively, shakes Rico's hand and exits all at the same time. "Thanks...I'll see you tomorrow."

After George exits, Rico looks sheepishly at John who is smiling broadly while leaning against the mirrored wall with his arms folded. John has given up on his student and sent him packing.

"If you keep giving away lessons like that. You're going to put Master Ozman out of business."

"Sorry. I can't help myself and I thought Hanshi would have done the same."

"I know and you're right. He reminded you of yourself when you were that age. I guess none of us paid cash for lessons in the old days and I thought that character building element of cleaning the dojo was a nice touch."

"Don't worry, I'll teach him myself and I promise it'll never happen again."

"Forget it. I've been known to do a few charity cases in my time. One more Mexican free loader around here isn't going to break the bank and besides, before you go," John adds. "I have a favor to ask of you."

"A favor? That's not like you, but as you know I'm into bartering. What do you need?"

"I need you to help an old friend of Hanshi." Just then, a woman walks into the dojo and Johnny indicates with a glance that this has something to do with *the old friend* and that he wants Rico to listen to what she has to say.

"I was sent here by a mutual friend of ours, Mr. Rose," An obvious attorney, who presented herself as Georgia Samuelson.

Ms. Samuelson was a knockout brunette right off the cover of Cosmopolitan. She was extremely well dressed, every hair was in place and her attitude was businesslike. She held a leather portfolio that was partially opened.

"Detective Rose doesn't have much time, but I asked him to listen your problem and see if he can help," Johnny shrugged and moved away, allowing Rico and Ms. Samuelson as much privacy as possible in the confines of the small office.

Johnny took a seat to the left of the desk, while Rico sat behind it. Samuelson was guided towards an empty chair at the center of the room. Before even crossing half the distance to the chair that had been set for her, she got right to her introduction, ignoring completely the formality of a handshake. Her curtness struck Rico as more rude than professional, and her impatience to proceed told him that, not only was she a lawyer, but that she felt utterly important and on a mission that somewhat embarrassed her.

"Have a seat Georgia. Relax," Rico smiled amiably and waved toward the chair, then ignored Ms. Samuelson. He was really just trying to shake things up by using her first name so quickly, and Johnny knew that there was nothing pressing and, therefore, no reason for Rico to keep the woman waiting. This too was somehow a ploy. Maybe Rico just didn't like her attitude and wanted to play with her a bit before cooperating.

The woman was a joy to look at, even with her personality flaws. Maybe Rico just wanted to keep her fragrance nearby. She made Johnny almost wish he needed a lawyer.

Rico spoke to himself, "I'm an active duty officer, but I do, on occasion take some private cases, many through referral from lawyers.

If I feel that the case might compromise my standing with the department, I refer it to a family member, my sister who is also a detective. Many of the cases I take involve someone needing to be located who isn't officially missing. Is that what this is?"

Rico shuffled through some papers for a moment then looked up, indicating he was now ready.

"That's a very astute observation," Samuelson began. "My client is a very well known celebrity. What I have to say to you is very confidential, for your ears only." Samuelson looked at Johnny.

"Mr. Angel is my closest associate. He's my *sensei* and that means that there is no one else I respect more. I tell him everything. He knows everything about all my cases. Think of him as me. Whatever you say will not go beyond this room."

The well placed complement had the desired effect. "Very well. If I have your personal assurance of complete confidentiality, my client's name is Marvin Masters. He has spent a considerable amount of money and time trying to locate *this* man."

Samuelson placed a photograph on Rico's desk. She had said Marvin Masters' name with great emphasis, assuming that Rico and Johnny would both be very impressed. Actually, they were impressed. Marvin Masters was considered one of the most influential men in the world. He had gained celebrity in Hollywood and turned millions of dollars and a knack for business into **billions** of dollars and one of the broadest financial portfolios that existed. What Ms. Samuelson did **not** understand was that, for all Rico's brilliance, he had no concept of celebrity. And, very well might not have ever heard of Marvin Masters.

This was born out by the fact that Rico did not even acknowledge the client's name, but picked up the photograph instantly, turning it over and considering it from all angles, as Samuelson proceeded.

"An attorney, Mr. Juan De La Rosa, recommended you as the very best missing person locator in the business. I personally do not see how you, or anyone can accomplish what teams of others have failed to, but Mr. Masters is desperate and willing to try anything."

"How old is this picture?" Rico asked, ignoring the lawyer's subtle insult.

"About six months old," Samuelson said.

"So this man has not been missing less than six months I assume."

"That is correct."

Rico turned the photo over and checked the back, then handed it to Ms. Samuelson. "What is the missing person's name?"

"His name is Joseph Turner."

"Pretty common name," Rico commented. "Do you know how old he is? Do you happen to have a date of birth, for instance?"

Samuelson reached into a folder and extracted the information that was requested, along with other pertinent data, as there was a history sheet already prepared.

"Why does Mr. Masters want to locate this man?" Rico's question was blunt, but anticipated.

"I'm sorry, but that is personal and cannot enter into your decision to take this case." You could see that Samuelson enjoyed being coy.

"Fine," said Rico. "In that case. I need one more piece of information. What is Mr. Masters' phone number? I mean, where can I contact him, right now?"

Now it was Samuelson's turn to be shocked. " I represent Mr. Masters' interests. For our purposes, you can consider him, *me*," using Rico's own words against him.

"You said that it's a personal matter. Well, I need to talk to the person that it matters to. You heard I was the best, and that is absolutely correct. If my associate and I decide to take this case, you will have no better chance of ever finding Joe Turner. But, you cannot interfere with my style. I don't want to hurt your feelings Ms. Samuelson, but I simply cannot take this case unless I talk to Masters."

Samuelson exhaled her resignation, leaned over and took Rico's phone from the receiver. Even that simple act was portrayed like a scene from a play, in which she seemed to feel she should be starring. After a dramatic interlude, the beautiful lawyer dialed a number and handed the phone to Rico.

Rico pressed the com-line button, so that all could hear the conversation.

"Mr. Masters?"

"Yes. Is this Rico Rose?"

"Yes it is, sir. I'm sorry to bother you, but it seemed wise to discuss my terms directly with you, considering the urgency that has been expressed."

"I've heard about you Mr. Rose and I was expecting your call," came the response.

"This is my fee sir; if I find your person, you pay me $10,000 for his whereabouts. If I don't find him, you pay me nothing."

There was a slight silence. "That seems fair. But, what do you think your chances are in finding Joe?"

"I don't like to take cases that I can't solve, Mr. Masters."

"Very well. How soon can I expect to hear from you?"

"If you remain at this number, I'll call you back in a few minutes to tell you what I know."

Now, Rico had a reputation for being able to get fast results, but Ms. Samuelson and Johnny were both surprised at the immediacy of this particular effort. They were also surprised when Rico asked them both to leave the room while he made a few calls.

"How long is this going to take?" Samuelson wanted to know.

"I have other clients to take care of."

"Just give me a few minutes, please," Rico said. "Mr. Angel will bring you up to date on our methods..."

He forced the two out the door and closed it. "So this is how he treats him...*self*?" asked Samuelson.

"There are times," Johnny said, "When I really don't *want* to know what's going on, but I just can't help myself." He looked at his watch. It was 11:15 in the morning. Samuelson was extremely displeased. They stood in horrible silence for what seemed like hours.

At precisely 11:30 A.M. the door to the office swung open and Rico stood there smiling.

"Please come back in." He waved them forward enthusiastically.

He was beaming. Johnny knew that something important was about to happen.

"Could you please get Mr. Masters on the telephone?" he directed Samuelson as soon as she entered. Samuelson obliged and again Rico put the conversation on the speaker.

"Mr. Rose?" Masters apparently hadn't given this number out much.

"Yes, sir. You are on speaker and I've located Mr. Turner."

"That's impossible." These words by Masters were barely audible and revealed a mixture of disbelief and skepticism.

"He's living at 27567 Forest Ave. in Tallahassee, Florida. He is using the name Joseph Tanner. He is willing to speak with you, thanks to a little coaxing on my part. I've talked with him at length, and, he's given me a number where you can call him. Is Ms. Samuelson empowered to write me a check?" The bluntness of Rico's statements made, even Johnny blush.

"Yes she is, Mr. Rose. But, how do I know that this is really Joe? I just have your word for it. I'll have to check out your findings before pay..."

Rico cut off Masters comments abruptly. "You know that I've found the right Turner, because he's the one who was screwing you in the backside, Mr. Masters. He was very explicit about your favorite positions during sex."

There was only a short pause, but it was a heavy one. Samuelson shook her head back and forth from John, to Rico and back again several times. Her face was one of sheer disorientation.

"You don't have much tact Mr. Rose, but, as you can hear, I'm telling Ms. Samuelson to make out a check." The phone went dead.

Samuelson removed a checkbook from her folder, filled in the amount agreed upon and handed it to Rico.

"Will there be anything else?" Rico said, with a totally straight face.

"No, thank you Mr. Rose. And, remember, everything that has taken place here today is to be held in the utmost confidence."

"Absolutely, Ms. Samuelson. But, I really have to ask you why Mr. Masters keeps such a beautiful lady lawyer around when he likes men so much?"

Samuelson turned and exited as quickly as she'd arrived. When they heard her car leave and knew she was no longer within listening distance, Johnny let out a yelp of exuberance.

"I can't believe it! $10,000 in fifteen minutes! How in the hell did you pull that one off? How did you find him? Is there going to be another celebrity sexually transmitted disease scandal in the news soon?" Johnny was filled with questions and admiration.

"As for your last question, I don't know. I hope not, but that may well be what is going on. Turner was just as worried about that as Masters was."

"And, what was that last thing with Samuelson? Why did you make that little comment about her boss?"

"Because she was lying from the time she walked in here. In fact, it was Samuelson who led me to Turner. "

"How could that be? She barely had anything to say to either one of us."

"That was the first thing that bothered me about her," Rico responded. "And, if I hadn't distrusted her, I might not have taken the time to look at the back of that photograph she gave me."

"What good did that do?" Now he really had Johnny going, but as usual, even when *the magician explained the magic* the audience was still impressed.

"She said they hadn't seen Turner for six months, but his photo was only two months old. She also did not seem to want me to learn anything. If investigators had been on this case for six months they must have learned something in that time, but she shared no information! Why was she trying to keep me from finding Turner? So, I just went to my sources in the phone company. I didn't *just* check Masters' conversations. I crossed-checked calls made by Masters with those made by Samuelson. Both had called Turner many times. Then, I checked for new numbers that had come TO Samuelson within the last two months. The numbers varied, but Florida kept coming up. I looked at the picture and realized that Turner was a typical surfer boy. If he left the West Coast he must have ended up in a warm place, like Florida. When I checked the directory with Samuelson's and Master's calls, Joe Tanner was the name in the book. It seemed more than coincidental that Joe Turner and Joe Tanner are very similar names, so I called the number."

"But, how did you know Masters' number?"

"That was the *super* easy part," Rico laughed. "Whenever someone dials a number it reads out right at the top of this phone here," he tilted the phone to show Johnny. "I was only worried I'd forget the number before I got you two out of the office."

"That was pretty smart, really, " Johnny conceded. "But, how did you know that Samuelson was lying? And, perhaps more importantly WHY was she lying? What did she have to gain?"

Rico's expression was half smile, half perplexity at his own ability. "That's something you're just are born with," he said, at last seeming to come to a satisfactory conclusion in his own mind. "I can just tell when someone is lying. At least, I *think* I can, and usually I'm right. What I need to do, and what I *DO* that others may not, is I go with what I feel.

In this case, my gut feeling was correct. And, for your last question I can only go with my feeling and piece it together with what I know from talking with Joe Turner. He didn't really tell me much, but it was clear that he had a relationship with Masters. When I told him I was a private investigator and that Mr. Masters was very interested in trying to find him, he's the one who brought up the sex thing. Turner was worried *he* may have gotten something from Masters. Then, Turner confirmed what I believed about Samuelson. He asked me why our Ms. Samuelson didn't tell him that Masters had been looking for him. My guess is that Samuelson was screwing Masters or Turner, either figuratively or literally, or both. After all, she IS a lawyer. Maybe there was a hustle going on, embezzlement, blackmail... or maybe it was a simple case of jealousy. In this business I've seen it all. And, now, I've seen how fast information can turn into $10,000. "

"But aren't you interested in finding out *all* the facts?"

"There are plenty of mysteries in life for us to be curious about," said Rico. "I do what I do, because I'm good at it, because it's in my blood. But, I'm also a professional." He thought a second, and then added with a boyish grin. "Now, if you should want to put up another $500, I'd be happy to invest a *whole day* into solving the entire mystery for you. I'll even answer all your questions."

"You still me much more than that for lessons! For now, let's just call it even-Steven."

"Don't worry, some of this money goes to the dojo. Wow, you really are a white guy…even Steven?"

A phone is ringing on the inside of Rico's apartment when he arrives home. Over the sound of the telephone we hear someone running to the door, finding keys and putting them into lock. The door opens to reveal Rico, just as the phone stops ringing. His facial expression is one of curiosity. In his hands he has his karate gear in a duffle bag. He pulls a belt holster out from under his shirt. Just as he sets it down, the phone begins to ring again. He reaches over and answers it.

"Hello?"

"Rico? This is Becky," a female at the other end responds.

"Becky?" Rico is tired and a little confused but something registers with his detective senses. "What's happened to Vito?"

Oddly composed, like someone who has been traumatized but is now numb from a prolonged period of hysteria Becky says, "He's dead, Rico. Vito's dead. I...I've been trying to call you all morning. Everyone's been trying to call you. He doesn't have any other family, but me. And you...you were like his brother. You gotta come over...I've been trying to call you all morning. Come on over, O.K.? He...I need you here."

"O.K. Becky. I'll leave right now." Rico doesn't wait for her response and can barely perceive the monotone, "goodbye" as he drops the receiver into its carriage.

After the phone is already in place, Rico speaks his final line to no one. "I'm sorry."

Turning, he looks to the wall and there is a picture of him and another man, Vito, the cop who had been killed. In the photo Rico and Vito are in police uniforms. They are smiling with arms around each other.

Rico remembers a time that he and his partner were together in the photo.

"You gotta be more careful, bro."

"Come on Panda Bear. You're too paranoid."

"In this business you've gotta be paranoid and it's just Panda, not Panda Bear. Don't you know anything about street-names?"

"Yeah, I'm interested in busting heroin dealers. So, I'm going undercover and my nickname's going to be Sleepy because that fits."

"Sleepy? Makes sense, but maybe you should call yourself Scaredy cause you worry so much. If you're too careful, you never get anything done."

"And if you're not careful you don't get a second chance, cause you're dead."

Rico is looking at the picture. He seems to get angry and sad at the same time. "That stupid jerk." He picks his keys up and heads out the door.

Rico is just coming out of his house and down walkway towards car. He gets into car and drives off, a few tears coming down his cheeks and he wipes them away as he drives. Rico begins to think back about his days in the Academy. Sounds and pictures from the past start to fill his head. He struggles to concentrate on his driving, but finally gives into the urge to drift into the past to erase the present.

Vito and Rico met in the Academy. The commanding officer was a hard ass and always kept the recruits standing, endlessly before releasing them to their assignments at the start of a long day, dragging out the last few moments in some sort of power trip. Standing at attention are Rico and Vito.

"Those are your assignments for the day, so if there are no questions I'll dismiss you to your duties." He looks around. "O.K., then..."

"Morelli!" Rico tries to disguise his voice to sound like a Mickey Mouse squeak, but everyone in line begins to laugh, in a controlled manner; Rico is motionless and expressionless. Vito is horrified. His last name is Morelli.

The C.O. is angry. "Everyone is dismissed...*but* you Rose. I want to see you in my office, *now*."

Later, in the locker room Rico walks past a group of men who stand around and talk quietly. As he approaches, they grow suddenly silent and look his way. One cadet walks up and initiates a conversation. "What the hell's the matter with you Rose?"

Rico shrugs and grins. "I'm just trying to make my time here memorable. Sorry, if anyone else got hurt."

"You're ruining it for everyone. We're getting sick of your screw ups. We don't care what kind of extra duty you've pulled from the ass of the CO…If you do this again, we're going to give you a lesson you *won't* just ignore."

All exit as Rico begins to change into his street clothes.

Vito steps out of the background as the others depart. "Why'd you have to chose *my* name? That's the thing that bothers me. We don't hardly even know each other."

"I can't help myself, Morelli," Rico says with a smile. "I just like you and I know we're going to be partners."

Vito seems not to be able to believe Rico's words, at first, then his face changes to anger and he slaps himself on the forehead. Slowly the two men begin to laugh and Rico imitates his performance from the parade ground.

"MORELLI!"

Both men laugh sophomorically and the thought of the laughter brings Rico back to the present. He is laughing while driving his car.

From inside the car Rico notices that he is driving through a red light. He swerves the car as if to miss traffic. To himself, under his breath he says, "Damn it."

He then looks into rear view mirror. There he sees the lights from a police motorcycle flashing him to the side of the road. He exhales, disgusted and makes appropriate motions to pull over.

A bike cop saunters up to the driver-side window, peering curiously. "Rico? Is that you?"

"Yeah, Hi Martin."

"Oh. I guess you know about Vito."

"Yeah, I'm on my way over to Becky's house right now."

"I...I just heard myself. Well. I'm sorry...Tell Becky, I'm sorry."

The two officers hardly have looked at one another and there is no mention of the red light.

Chapter Three
A Game of Tag

In a nice suburban home, there is a knock at the door, and a woman comes to answer it. This is Becky, Vito's widow. She is about thirty, black hair and a good figure. She speaks to the door, not yet opening it. "Who is it? Rico?"

From the other side, "Yeah."

The door is opened slowly.

"Come in."

"Are you alright?" She closes the door, leaving Rico to stand awkwardly in the entry, just behind her for a moment.

Then, turning, "I'm O.K...now. It's just..." She breaks down completely, letting the tears flow freely as Rico holds her. She cries for several seconds and then seems to get a hold of herself.

Becky pushes herself away. "Thanks." She walks from the entry way and Rico follows, looking at her with curiosity. They make it to the living area.

She sits and her air is very controlled.

Cautiously Rico breaks the silence, "Do you want to talk now?"

"I wouldn't mind it."

"Do you want to talk about Vito?"

Deliberating, then with confidence Becky responds, "I *need* to."

Apologetically, Rico proceeds, "Hey, I don't know what good it's going to do. I just want to know what happened. Maybe I'll feel better if I know. Maybe talking will make us both feel better."

"Of course he wanted me to tell you *everything*. That was always an agreement we'd had. *'If anything happens to me, tell Rico,'* he said. So, I'm telling you. He was killed on the streets. Those damn streets that you both seem to love. I don't have all the details yet. Polonowski and McCoy found him. He was in an alley, stabbed…brutally stabbed. Maybe it was a user. Maybe it was a dealer who made him as a cop. Like you said, what difference does it make?"

Rico's eyes begin to well and redden with tears. "I don't know…" Rico changes the subject and his attitude, as he is obviously trying to cheer up Becky. "Hey, remember the first time you and me and Vito and Susie went out together?"

She relaxes. "You two were so ridiculous, so proud to finally be cops. You couldn't give it up, even for one night."

"You have to admit it was a fun date though."

"Yeah. I was kind of bored until that little kid came running up, what was his name?"

"Joey."

Rico and Becky start to recall the night at the makeshift, small-scale dance and carnival, in a local church parking lot. The four (Vito, Becky, Susie and Rico) were sitting at a table, talking and laughing as a little boy, about ten, runs up to the table. The boy's name was Joey.

"Hey Panda. You want to bust somebody right now?"

"What's going down Joey?"

Proudly," Some cholo is messing up some dude's lock, out in the parking lot." Joey points.

The four at the table looked uncomfortably at each other. Becky spoke with resignation in her voice. "Go ahead. You can't let a car get stolen right under your noses. How would that look on your Super cop's resume?"

Rico and Vito nodded to each other and smile playfully; Suddenly, they jumped from their seats and into action. Slamming on the breaks, Rico and Vito slowed and sneaked into the parking lot. There were about a dozen kids following behind them. Rico waved them back with his hand. Joey, among them, acknowledged that he understands and takes control of the group. Vito moves off in one direction, at a crouch. Rico moves directly into the cars.

In midst of cars Rico, with his gun out, huddles near a V.W. Bug, listening. He can hear the sound of metal scraping against metal. He peers up. Over his shoulder we see Vito in the distance, coming from the opposite direction. There is a youth prying, amateurishly at a car door with a long, thin metal bar. He is only a few cars away from Rico. Suddenly, he seems to sense another's presence and turns. He sees Rico, drops the Slim-Jim and begins to run.

Rico, standing, hollered, "Halt. I'm a police officer." Then, looks disgusted and gestures his frustration by jumping up and beginning to run. Vito is seen running in from the other direction and a short chase scene follows.

Vito and Rico close in on the suspect who is totally panicked and begins to check the doors of the other autos that he passes, one after another. Finally, a door opens to him and he jumps in.

Vito and Rico arrived at the escape vehicle to the sound of a blood-curdling scream. This scream is mixed with the sounds of a dog's growls and the tearing of flesh and clothing. The would-be car thief has jumped into a car that had a Doberman pinscher in it. The big animal is mauling the boy as Rico and Vito watch through the window. There is a moment of indecision. Rico turned to Vito and said, smiling, "Don't you just hate it when that happens?"

Back at Becky's house, Becky and Rico are laughing mildly over their reminiscences.

"I wonder what ever happened to that guy."

"I don't know. Maybe he became an animal trainer."

"I don't think we even arrested him!"

Changing the subject suddenly, Becky adds, "You know, there's one thing that sticks in my mind about what Vito's been involved with for the past month or so. I didn't tell anyone else about it...well, because I wasn't sure if it meant anything and you know Vito. He asked me not to talk to anyone except you about his work."

"What is it?"

"He didn't tell me about specific things, but there was something that was eating at him. Some sort of name kept coming up into his investigation he was on and he didn't know what to make of it."

"What was the name?"

Trying hard to remember, "I think it was Paloma. I'm not sure. I don't think it had any connection to what he was working on but, he kept hearing it. Maybe that's why it bothered him. He said it had something to do with *a game of tag*. Do you know what he was talking about?"

"It's a technique we used to run down leads, but I'm not sure this is the time to tell you about it."

"Even though it hurts right now, I'm a cop's widow. That means that I used to be a cops wife. I'd like to hear, if you don't mind. Maybe I'll be able to put something else together for you."

"O.K. then…You remember how Vito used to say that 'there aren't as many *Kojaks* and *Columbos* on the cop's side as there are *Jesse Jameses* and *Pancho Villas* on the law-breaker's side?" Rico was trying to make a point.

"I don't remember those exact words, but it sounds like something either one of you might have said."

"In other words, a person really doesn't have to be that smart to be a decent and successful cop. Primarily, they just have to be honest. But, it's necessary to possess a certain amount of cleverness to be a good criminal."

"So the criminals are smarter?"

"I don't want you to think that Vito admired The Bad Guys, or that he thought that The Good Guys are stupid," Rico added. "I just want you to see where this is coming from. The bad guys spend all their time thinking about ways to break the law. Lawmen are at a disadvantage. I understand that being a good cop is like being good at math, while being good at crime requires more creativity. But, being a *great* cop...now that requires a little more skill and a lot of luck."

Rico's perspective did show a philosophical yet factual approach to the business of hunting down criminals and it took Becky's mind off of the fact that her husband had just been killed. In one sense, this philosophy was overly simplistic. Good guys did good and he (Rico) and Vito were good guys. Bad guys did bad things. The good guys put the bad guys behind bars. That was their job. That was how the game was played.

Most importantly, *all* of the players weren't that smart. In fact, Vito and Rico used to howl with laughter at the severity of stupidity in some of the crimes that were committed. In the end, good just went on opposing evil. That was the way it was. It was simple, but it was a perspective that was workable.

So, realizing this difference between the two species, Rico and Vito neatly fit themselves into the structure. Logic followed that the worse the bad guy was who they arrested, the better it would be for the good guys.

"The criminal justice system is filled with games," Rico went on. "Some really stupid rules. Now, we have the Three Strikes Rule, plea bargaining, Miranda Rights violations. If the ball isn't hit in the air, and the cops forget to touch all the bases then the victims lose twice. The criminals are never prosecuted."

"What about violations of the rights of the innocent? What about the victims, the family of the victims?" Becky asked, taking a *hypothetical* and turning it into a *personal*.

"That's not what I'm talking about. It's one thing to make laws to protect the innocent, but we accidentally make them to protect the guilty as well. Criminals find loopholes and try to cheat. We accept that and we looked at tracking down the bad guys like *A Game Of Tag*. That's where one bad guy leads us to another and we see where the trails cross and then we find another bad guy crossing at the same place and so on. Vito was not one for explaining things. He much rather wanted to demonstrate. And, that was the case one Halloween, when Vito had taken me into the suburbs to watch over some kids. We had driven into an area where a family was presenting a Haunted House for local children to participate in. It was a nice gesture. The family was one of those civic-minded few that also lit the house to the hilt and set up an impressive nativity scene during Christmas time, and sprang for a few extra sparklers on the 4th of July. There was never any charge and for no other reason than they felt like doing something fun for their neighbors. *'Which one are we watching'* I asked after a short span of diligently observing, kids coming and going with smiles, but always leaving with a piece of candy. Vito looked at me and smiled. '*We're watching all of them,*' he said."

"Oh, I get it. Trust NO one!" Becky said, being a little sarcastic.

"No, I asked the same question, but Vito told me that he *trusted everyone*, until they did something to lose that trust.*"

"I think this sounds more like you than Vito," Becky said pointedly. "I'm really not sure HOW you arrive at your conclusions sometimes, and Vito was always talking about you like you are some sort of savant. It seems like some of the worst people in the world are your most trusted allies, while the most innocent looking are suspect from the very beginning."

"Well, after a while, two partners start to think alike. I'm not sure what came first, all I know is that it is how we both thought. You and Vito probably influenced each other in ways that you might now see, yet. Being a close partner is a lot like being married. We were talking about *A Game of Tag*."

"Yes, I remember, but so far I'm not sure what that means."

"It's like this. If we look at crime and punishment as a game, then there are other games that can be associated to it."

"In what way?"

"Well, let's think about any other sport...what's your favorite?"

"I can tolerate baseball."

"O.K. baseball. Who do baseball players like to hang around with?"

"Hey, I didn't know I was going to be tested!" Becky argued.

"Come on, give me some help here."

"Alright, I'd say that ball players generally hang out with other ball players and car racers hang out with other car racers...I think I see where you're going with this."

"Right! So cops like cops and criminals are forced to hang with other members of their own team."

"So, what's the deal? What does that have to do with Tag?"

"It's just a little game we play, kind of like tracking backwards, with a twist."

"So now you're Daniel Boone?"

"If Daniel was Jewish and Mexican, I'd be a lot like him. But, what I mean is that, if you ARE tracking you can follow your quarry forward to find what is making the tracks, or you can follow them backwards to see where the animal STARTED from."

"I'm with you so far, Dan'l."

"But what about those times when the tracks you are following cross other tracks? What do you do then?"

"There you go with the tests again," Becky said in mild protest.

"So, I'm going to answer your question with a question...Are you back tracking for a reason? I mean, are you trying to find something in particular? Or, are you just following tracks for the hell of it?"

Rico thought a moment and responded, "A little of both. That time, on Halloween we were watching the kids for protection. Then, all of a sudden Vito said to me pointing to one of the parents, '*Look at that guy. He's loaded,*' I was astounded by his observation, because I was usually the one to spot things like this. There was this guy, about twenty or so was walking toward the park with a young woman I took to be his wife, and a small child, I believed to be his son. He was walking normally, not weaving or swaying, talking to the woman at his side, and both were smiling amiably. However, it was obvious to both of us that he was stoned."

"Why? Why did you think he was stoned? And, why would you care?"

"It was Halloween and the kid was obviously ready to trick-or-treat, but Dad had led him here, to this particular house and they weren't going inside. It just wasn't right."

"So, what happened next?"

"We decided that we *could* bust this guy or we could follow a new trail to maybe a bigger bust. Following the other kids had led us to this guy, his wife and his son. Following any one of these three could lead us in a whole new direction that might be better. As it turned out, Vito and I had to separate because *Papa,* all of a sudden meets another guy, kisses his lady and the little boy and rushes off. The mom, on the other hand doesn't just go back to trick-or-treating, but stands there and waits, like she's waiting for someone. Vito went off and followed the dad who was later busted making a delivery with the other guy. I stayed and followed the mom and son. We found out that the kid was the key to another illegal operation. He didn't have just candy in his bag, but was carrying heroin!"

Becky rolls her eyes. There's a short span of silence then she asks, "Rico? What are we going to do *now*?"

As if from dream, "I can help you with the funeral, that sort of thing if you need me."

"I mean, what're we going to do about Vito's being dead, about finding his killer?"

"I don't know exactly, Becky, but Vito wanted me to see where this Paloma character's tracks lead and whose tracks cross his. Vito thought it was an important enough lead to tell you about it, just in case. Other than that, I don't know. You know I'll do what I can. I'll find out who it was. I'll find out who this Paloma character is, I promise." This seems to be all that Becky wanted to hear for now. She stands as if this is Rico's cue to leave.

"Can I use your phone?"

"Sure."

"I want to call Susie." Rico explains, although Becky had already stopped listening. "I haven't talked to her today. She must be wondering..." Becky waves him off with a nod, picks up a nearby phone and hands it to Rico.

He dials. "Hi, Hon? It's Rico."

The voice at the other end can be heard by Becky. "Where the hell'uve you been? You know I can't stand it when you don't call and let me know you're alright."

"Hon. Listen, Vito's been killed."

"Oh, God. I'm sorry."

"I just found out about it a little while ago. I'm over at Becky's. I didn't have a chance to call."

Susie's attitude changes, "It's alright. We can talk later. How's Becky?"

"Alright, you know. I'd like to come over, now, if it's not to late."

"Sure. Come on. Are you leaving Becky now?"

"Yeah. I guess so."

"Can I talk to her?"

Turning to Becky, "Susie wants to know if you'd like to talk?"

Becky quietly takes the phone and Rico stands for a few seconds watching. She begins to cry and he, becoming uncomfortable, exits.

A number of officers and plain-clothes detectives sit at desks, crammed in close quarters. They are all busy at various office tasks. After this is established, Rico enters with an angry and determined look on his face. Many stop and look at him as he walks through the desks. A plain-clothes officer turns to another and comments as Rico walks directly into a door marked "Chief Sheer."

"More *oso* than Panda," the officer comments.

Another man nods and smiles. We see the office door slam and the cops cringe.

Rico enters and the sound of the door slamming punctuates his arrival. The Chief is a gnarly looking guy, about fifty years old. He doesn't even respond to Rico's entrance. He is on the telephone and talking casually. He doesn't even look up. Rico stands in front of the desk for a few seconds, boldly then he relaxes slightly.

The Chief speaks into the receiver, extremely casually, "I'll have to call you back. Something's just come up. O.K. goodbye." He hangs up and turns to Rico. "So, you're Rico Rose."

"That's right sir. I thought you knew me. I'd like to ask a favor."

"Ask away."

"I'd like to have Morelli's cases."

"Yes." More to himself, then to Rico, "I've heard about you Rose. You make some good arrests and then get an awful lot of complaints."

"I get my share of both sir. But, if I wasn't making the busts then the bad guys wouldn't be making the complaints."

"I suppose that's true." He regroups and continues. "So you want Morelli's cases. Any particular reason, I'm obliged to ask, as if it's not obvious?"

"Honestly? Yes sir. I'd like to find the guys who killed him."

With feigned indignation, "Personal vendetta? That's the kind of thing that ruins your reputation."

"Not a vendetta, a promise I made to his wife, sir."

"Don't you think that homicide is better equipped to handle this?"

"No sir, I don't. I know the streets. I know how to work the streets. Vito and I worked dope together and I learned to think like him. It's a different kind of world for the dopers and cops working undercover. I know how to live in that world and to think like them."

Somewhat shocked the Chief responds, "Well...what if there aren't any cases to assign you? What if Detective Morelli was on one of his rogue missions that you undercover cops are famous for, the ones that go nowhere that anyone can see but you?"

"I'll take my chances. I'd just like to be involved from the end that I'd best be able to work from. I don't want to get in anyone's way. I'm willing to work with homicide. I'll let them know if something's going down."

"That's very big of you Rose, but I'll have to think about it. Why don't you take a day or two off? I'm sure you could use some time to think about things and to help the grieving widow."

"I'd like to get started on this right away, sir and I know that is the widow's wish as well."

"Take a couple of days anyways. I don't want to know how you spend your time. Do whatever you like, but officially, you're not involved."

Rico turns to walk out the door.

"And Rose?"

Rico stops.

"Don't get in any trouble. And by that I mean don't do anything stupid, or alone that is going to get *you* killed. I can't risk losing two hard workers. I'll let you know when I've made a decision that concerns you."

Rico turns away and opens door, but before leaving turns back and asks, "Sir?"

The chief looks up.

"If I don't get this assignment, I'll be forced to resign."

Looking back down, "I understand."

Rico exits.

The chief lifts the receiver on the phone/com on his desk. "Nancy? Get Lieutenant Barnes in here right away will you? Oh, and Nancy, pull the jacket on officer Rico Rose."

Rico is just driving away from the station. He picks up the microphone in his car, waits, then asks for an open line, giving the dispatcher a number. After a moment, a woman's voice answers at the other end, "The Flower Shop."

"Hi. This is Rico. Can I talk to Susie?"

"I'm sorry Rico. Susie is sick today. She's at home."

"Oh, O.K. I'll call her there." Hangs up.

In the chief's office, Lieutenant Barnes, a sixty-ish, slightly overweight, tall black man comes in. "What's up?"

"Oh! I'm thinking about giving Rose a green light on following up Morelli's cases. What do you know about him?"

"Oh, so that's what that was all about. I don't know much I'm afraid. I saw him once or twice at the academy. He was kind of an oddball, screwed up some, but I hear he's a real worker now. I think he got Police Officer of the Year for three years in a row."

"What do you make of this?" The Chief asked, handing the file to Barnes.

Looking over file, "Several commendations...Officer of The Year...Oh, yeah. Shotgun Rose. I remember that. He practiced with the shotgun the same way everyone else practiced with their revolvers. He always seemed to have his gun propped onto his hip. At the Academy, we had him in an approach and pullover simulation. Sarge Bender was always riding him, told him specifically he *wasn't going to have to shoot this time*."

"What happened?"

Smiling, "Bender was wrong. The officer who was playing the suspect was a woman. Rose had her get out of the car and she had forgotten to take off her gun. He told her to lie down on the ground. It was about ninety degrees and the asphalt was hotter than hell. She jumped back and started wiping her hands on her skirt."

"And?"

"Rose had valid cause to believe that she was going for her weapon, so he shot her. It drove Bender crazy."

"I see. It was a *righteous simulated shooting* then?"

"Well, what would you have done?"

The chief simply nods his head, knowingly.

"If you want to find out anything else, I think he's partners with Sullivan and I know Sergeant Berman works with him sometimes."

"O.K., see what you can find out. I think I might give him what he wants."

"We don't really have leads, so we don't have anything to lose, I guess."

Susie is a young, fairly good-looking *chicana* sitting in front of a television. Her hair is disheveled; her eyes are red. She looks as though she's been crying. There's a knock at the door. A young man comes from behind Susie, who doesn't move. This is her brother, Poncho. "Hey sis, Rico is here."

Rico is holding a bouquet of flowers and speaks directly to Poncho, "Thanks, bro."

"Hey, Rico!" He directs Rico toward Susie with a tilt of his head. "I think you better see what's wrong there." Poncho exits.

"Hi, Hon. What're you doing at home today?"

Not looking up, Susie responds, "I didn't feel like working today."

"Are you sick?" Rico sits next to her and moves closer, as if to examine.

Susie moves away, "In a way." Rico stops his pursuit to listen, "I'm sick of being the girlfriend of a cop."

Rico stands dumbly for a moment, without expression. Susie looks toward him, defiantly waiting for his response.

"Do we have to get into this again...now?"

"Yes, goddamn it. We have to get into this, *now*." She stands and faces Rico. "I can't take this anymore." Calculating her next words she adds. "I just don't *want* to love you anymore. I don't want to get a call in the middle of the night that you've been stabbed to death by one of those slimy scum that you think are your friends. You spend more time with those people then you spend with me."

"Those people have got to trust me or they won't tell me anything!"

"They don't give a damn about you. Don't you realize that? You're not a god, or some kind of superhero that everyone on the street owes something to. You're just a cop. You're their enemy. And, they're going to kill you someday, just like they killed Vito. I don't want to be around to see it."

"Listen you little bitch, you think like that because you're one of those people that hate cops; you 're one of the scum of the streets. I don't know why I ever tried to lift you out of the gutter...perezosa." Susie sits back down in front of the television. She speaks vacantly, as if to herself, "Perezosa...bitch are not names that you call the person you love or allow someone you love to call you."

Rico storms to the door. Susie never looks up from the television or changes her blank expression.

Chapter Four
The Value of a Friend

Rico enters the karate studio. Johnny is sitting at the desk, in the small entrance/office; he looks up when Rico enters and seems surprised.

"Didn't you get enough this morning? Aren't you tired?" Then, as if coming to a realization, "Hey, by the way, thanks for helping with that Masters thing."

Rico looks less than welcoming as he walks past Johnny, directly into the dojo. He removes his shoes and bows before his feet touch the floor, but without changing his street clothes, he begins to pound away at the heavy bag and John rises to walk over and watch. After we get to see a few well-placed kicks and punches, John comments. "Hey Rico?"

Not stopping,"Yeah?"

"You're a cop right?"

"Yeah, you know I'm a cop."

"Isn't there a law against destruction of property?"

Now Rico stops, "Yeah, why?"

"Then you better stop hitting my bag like that or I'll have to file a complaint." slowly Rico smiles and exhales a small gust of wind that resembles a laugh.

"That was the slowest and smallest laugh one of my jokes ever got. What's bothering you?"

"It's a terrible world."

"That's kind of a strong statement, especially from you. Don't you think? Is it Susie, or the cop business?"

"A friend of mine got killed yesterday."

"On the street?"

"Undercover cop. You know, Vito. He came in here a few times with me."

Johnny is taken aback. "Wow, this is heavy. I don't think I ever met anyone that got killed before."

"It happens to cops all the time, more often than people think."

"So, that's why you're trying to kill this bag?"

"It helps me think, but you were more right than you thought. Susie and I just had a fight, too."

"Sometimes I hate my psychic abilities. How bad?"

"She says it's over. I said a few things I regretted as soon as the words came out of my mouth. You know."

"Does she realize what a great detective you are? That was really impressive how you figured that whole thing out yesterday."

"I was pretty impressed with myself until this thing with Vito and with Susie. Now, I've got new concerns and it's harder when the person you are trying to locate, doesn't want to be found."

"You mean like bad guys trying to hide out?"

"Sometimes," Then, as if realizing something, "And other times it's important to know that whatever the reason, people who hide all have some common connections."

"I don't get it."

"I didn't until just this minute either. There was something else bothering me and I didn't know what do to until you saved the day once again Sensei."

"Always glad to be of service. What did I do this time?"

"Vito's wife said he gave her a message for me."

"What does it mean?"

"He told her to tell me that, if anything happened to him to remember a name and A Game of Tag."

"I'm not sure how we got here, but talking seems to be help you. I'm happy to take some credit, so keep going."

"That game related to a bust we did later, that was as simple as the first rule of economics…supply and demand. I was helping him with a stakeout a while back and he we busted some heavy-hitters because they were operating out of a warehouse."

"So?"

"So, there were a bunch of deliveries going *in*, but nothing ever seemed to get produced at that business. Nothing ever came *out*. So we knew that they were producing something that didn't get shipped in the usual way. What we didn't know what was going on, but we knew it wasn't *business as usual*, because the usual business operates on one simple principle…"

"Oooohhh, supply and demand!"

"Right, someday I'll let you ride along with me and show you what I mean. For now, though I'm not sure *who* I'm looking for, but I know that I'm looking for someone who is trying *not* to get found. So, certain principles apply. See?"

"I'm with you…in principle, but I'm not sure where you're going with this."

"Believe it or not, because of what you just said, I'm going to head over and talk to a crying Israeli mother and father. You can come along, if you like, but if you haven't spent much time around Jewish people, this might not be a good introduction."

"Why for you say this, my little mashugina? Do I look like a goya or something? I can't wait to find out what one thing has to do with the other?"

"Vito had asked me to talk to these people a few weeks ago, kind of like you asked me to talk to Samuelson yesterday. He told me they were very upset, because they've lost, not one but, *two* daughters to the lure of U.S. freedom."

"Their little girls were kidnapped?"

"No, they ran away after getting into the wrong crowds."

"How are you going to find them? And, how is finding them going to help you find Vito's killer?"

"Good questions," Rico said, then added, "...and probably ones that Mom and Dad will want to ask also. I can only hope that Vito's killer, involved with drugs and hiding, has been running in the same crowds as the two Israeli princesses who are doing the same things. I think I should go and meet these people before I decide."

With that, they closed shop, which involved stacking papers from one place to another on the already messy desk, and jumped into Rico's car.

Along the way, to Johnny's surprise, Rico dropped off the highway into a rather seedy area of town and pulled into an alleyway. As they drove down the alley, between two rows of houses, Johnny noticed that the activity at the rear of the houses was much more pronounced than one would have suspected from the front of the buildings. Men were working on cars, children played and women walked and talked.

"Doesn't anyone use the front door around here?" Johnny asked.

"Not unless *immigra* is at the backdoor," Rico joked, as we pulled up to a group of men surrounding several broken down autos.

"Hey, Henry!" Rico called out to a pair of legs that stuck out from beneath a '57 Chevrolet.

"Panda! What's happening?" came the enthusiastic response, as *Henry* pushed his way out from beneath the vehicle. "Gimme' a bear hug *carnal*." A mid-twenties looking Hispanic man came toward them as they exited Rico's Camaro.

"Keep those goddamn greasy arms off me, you asshole," was Rico's reply. Both men were smiling broadly, the most amiable and friendly relationship was obvious.

"So what do you need Panda my man? A free tune-up?"

"Not today," said Rico. "I just wanted to know if you wanted to make a little extra money *por su familia*."

"You know me," answered Henry, with a coy shrug. "Who do I got to take down?"

"For reals man," Rico laughed along with the other men who still continued to work on their various cars. "This gig's legit. Is the Limo ready to ride? I may need a driver and a car for a few days for a couple of folks in Canoga Park."

"Sure man! I'm always ready to help out...and to make a few extra dollars. Just let me know what you need. But, why don't you just let this vato play chauffeur?" He tilts his head toward John. "Is he one of your *jooda* playmates?" This was Henry's way of saying that he didn't know Johnny and didn't feel comfortable talking in front of him.

"Firme bro', this is my sensei. I bring him around to show him interesting characters like you and the other vatos here." All the gang gave John a brief cheer, and he bowed low, like an actor to an audience. "Besides," added Rico. "The *hombre* can kick anybody's ass, but he can't drive for shit. He's like an old lady!" Everyone found this statement to be utterly hilarious, especially when Rico pantomimed

Angel, hunched over behind the wheel of a car, while he added kung fu fighting sounds to the characterization.

"Don't worry *viejo*," Henry interrupted finally. "There aren't many of us who can drive crazy enough for Ricardo here."

When Rico and Johnny left, even though Johnny had been the object of humor, he felt much more comfortable in the area and related this fact to Rico, asking finally, "Why'd we stop there in the first place?"

"Don't know," Rico said honestly. "I just thought I might need a driver. Jews hate to drive themselves. I know. I'm Jewish. I grew up with Jews. And, Henry is always looking to make some extra bucks for him family. I try to keep him busy, that way he doesn't go back to this former job. Henry has two very special talents. "

"One is cars, right?"

"Right, he's the best mechanic in the business. I've had him build cars for me from nothing. In fact, the car we're riding in now used to be a pile of parts."

"And, what's his other talent? Something illegal no doubt."

"No doubt. But, you'd never guess by looking at him. That's your clue. Do you want to play detective?"

"O.k.," Johnny said. "Since he's healthy looking and had that great friendly smile, I'd have to guess that he's not into drugs, but maybe he's a con man, though he obviously doesn't mind getting his own hands dirty."

"You're partly right and partly wrong," Rico said as we pulled to a stop in front of a suburban home in a much nicer neighborhood. "He's not into drugs, but his crimes USED to be much more serious. Henry was one of the best contract hit men in the business...or so the story goes. There were never any convictions. I met and busted him, but there was no evidence against him."

"So, the mechanic was a *mechanic*."

Rico laughed and disappeared out of the car before John could question him any further about this Henry. Henry certainly didn't look anything like the typical hit man that he'd come to visualize from many years of T.V. and mobster movies. If this *was* the truth, it explained why everyone laughed at Henry's initial comments to Rico.

In a moment, Johnny found himself standing at a door, knocking, as a shiver ran through his body. Rico stood back and to one side, and John realized that it was a much safer place to stand then right at the center of the door where he was.

"Don't embarrass me, Special Agent," Rico said, slyly as the door was opened and Rico moved in front of Johnny. "Hello, I'm Rico Rose. This is Special Agent Johnny Angel," his introduction was made immediately, in a totally professional tone, to a rather burly looking old gentleman wearing a beret. All Johnny could do was smile and nod.

They were led inside, without a word, into a large living area. Two people, a middle-aged man and woman, were seated on a sofa and directed Rico and John to sit in two empty chairs that faced them from across a coffee table. Rico jumped right in to a Yiddish explanation of who Johnny was. Johnny only surmised this because occasionally Rico would point to Johnny casually and nod or laugh.

"Meir zayn asked keyn kumen aher un zen az meir zol helfn gefinen dayn daughters [We were asked to help find your daughters]," Rico surprised everyone with his fluent Yiddish.

"Meir zayn zogn vegn`du nu du bist a yid? [We knew you were coming. Are you a Jew]" The mother was the first to speak.

"Ye` al-pi mine barmitzva [Yes, according to my barmitzva]."

"Yenik iz der moger kid? Err iz nisht a yid iz err? [Who's the skinny kid. He's not a Jew, is he?]" It was the father's turn to speak.

"Neyn, he's mine bodyguard. Err kenen hargen`du mit zayn hands un feet. Nu, velkh kenen`du zogn undz yener vel helfn undz gefinen dayn daughters? [No, he's my bodyguard. He can kill you with his hands and feet. So, what can you tell us that will help us find your daughters?]"

Rico had put the parents at ease and now the three, all great friends now, broke into English to include Johnny in the conversation.

"We think they are still in the Valley, maybe moving between somewhere around here and Hollywood," said the father. At the mention of Hollywood, the mother's countenance sagged, as if she'd been wounded.

"None of their friends that we know have heard from them in weeks, but some of the wilder girls…you know the ones who are not Jewish, say they've seen them in the company of drug users."

"Hob`du hern abi specific names? Hob`du hern fun yeder heysn Paloma? [Have you heard any specific names? Have you heard of anyone called Paloma?]" Rico wanted to know.

"No, we don't know anything specific. I'm afraid we haven't been much help."

Rico begins to move away with John following close behind, but with obvious reluctance. "Don't worry. It doesn't sound like they are in any great danger. We'll do what we can to find them and I'll let you know if anything comes up."

"And, what about the chauffer?" Johnny felt compelled to comment before they were completely out the door. Rico looked back and noticed that Johnny's words had piqued the couple's interest.

"Ye`mine bodyguard reminds mir yener meir visn fun a driver yenik kenen help`du arayn dayn shver mol. Ikh bin zikher nisht hobn dayn daughters aher keyn helfn aroys has makhn khayes der iker shver for`du. [Yes, my bodyguard reminds me that we know of a driver who can help you in your difficult time. I'm sure not having your daughters here to help out has made life especially hard for you.]

The couple just nodded their approval and seemed to hold Johnny in much higher esteem than they had previously. Rico now forced a quick exit and just outside Johnny continued, "You know what I'd like to hear? I'd like to hear the story of how you and Susie met."

"Why now?"

"You know that remembering tiny details is part of your martial arts training. I'd like to hear about the time with Susie, that is furthest away from your most recent time with your fight. Maybe we can find out what to do, or find out if there *is* anything to do..."

"I don't think you're going to give me any choice."

"That's right."

Rico lifts his gaze, as if remembering and begins to recount his and Susie's first meeting. "I was already working plain clothes and I got a call from this store owner that he had a kid, a shoplifter, he wanted me to come and scare. The kid was trying to get a can of spray paint, you know, the silver-metallic kind for sniffing purposes and the guy caught him." Rico relates the incident that took place in a small store in San Fernando. *When Rico arrived he found a little Chicano kid, about eight years old, sitting in a chair and an older man, also Chicano standing watch over him. The boy looked tough, but scared. He was watching the man's movements with interest, when Rico entered, looking grubby looking, with dirty clothes and a two-day beard. The storeowner signaled with his head as Rico entered and Rico knew that this was the boy in question.*

Rico called to the boy, "Hey, es'ay, what's your name?"

The boy didn't answer, so the storeowner responded for him. "His name is Juanito Carlos."

"I'm police officer Rose," Rico introduced himself, taking out his badge to show it to the boy. "I'd like you to come with me." Rico took the boy by the arm with a wink to the storeowner. The boy was terrified.

Rico walked Juanito out of the store through the back door. When the two got into the alley Juanito looked around, obviously growing more and more frightened and concerned.

"Hey, where's your cop car?"

"Oh, we might not make it to the car. I want to see how tough you are first."

The boy's eyes widened and his lips parted slightly as his lower jaw edged downward.

"You ever hear of the Panda?" The boy shook his head indicating he hasn't. "You're not as street-smart as I thought you were. Well, I'm the Panda. You know why they call me the Panda?"

The boy shook his head in the negative.

"Because, even though I'm cute and cuddly looking, when someone makes me mad, I go out of control, just like a bear. I'll pull your arms right off your body." Rico makes a gesture like he's pulling Juan's arms off, one at a time. "But, there are nice bears and I can be that kind of bear too. If you do good, then I'm good to you. Comprende?"

Juanito shook his head in the affirmative, this time.

"Why don't you just arrest me right away? Or, you could just let me go," Juanito suggested.

"Why are you so anxious to go to the joint fella?

Juanito took on a tough affect once again, "Prison's not so bad."

Rico got curious, "Oh, you've been down? What was the beef?"

Somewhat proudly, Juanito responded, "My dad's been there plenty of times. He says you gotta be macho to make it in prison. He say's that doing drugs is O.K. with him too."

"Your dad's a user?"

"Sure. I've seen him do it too, hundreds of times. I..."

Rico was fed up with the little tough guy act and interrupted.

"Listen you little pendejo, I'm goin' to put it to you straight. Your father's an asshole and you're a bigger goddamn asshole than he is because you want to go nowhere. Stealing is against the law and jails are the most miserable places on Earth!" Rico was beside himself with distain now and barely took a breath before continuing. "Being a drug user is bad enough, but people who steal or hurt anyone else in any way to feed their habit to use, especially if they are nothing but a "sniffer." Those are the lowest form of slime that there is on Earth." Rico picked the boy up by the front of shirt and looked directly into his eyes. "If I ever HEAR of you doing anything wrong again, spitting on the sidewalk, jaywalking, missing school or even farting in public, I guarantee you'll regret it. You'll never make it to prison because I doubt that you'll even make it to the hospital. Comprende?"

Suddenly, before the boy has a chance to answer, a purse drops from above and strikes Rico from behind. He cringes a few times and then turns, using the boy as a shield. Turning, Rico sees a younger version of Susie. She has seen the tail end of the interrogation and has misinterpreted what is going on here.

"You bully! Intimitar, leave that little one alone, before I call the cops! Police! Police!"

Rico puts Juanito down and the boy immediately takes off running.

Now, he turns to face Susie and pulls out his badge while he is still being struck repeatedly.

"I am a cop," he says casually, between blows.

Susie, abruptly stops striking Rico, puts her purse over her shoulder and begins to straighten her hair. "I...I thought you were...I didn't..."

While putting away the badge, he responds, "Forget it. It's all right. If more people were like you we might have less crime." He stops and thinks about what he just said then adds, "But we might have more people getting killed for butting in where they shouldn't. You could've gotten killed! What if I was some banger?"

Embarrassed and also flirtatious, Susie allows Officer Rose to council and reprimand her for taking chances.

"So what happened next?" John was totally immersed in Rico's tale of how he met Susie.

"I asked her if she had anything against going out with cops; she said she didn't, and I got her phone number."

"You asked her if she had anything against going out with cops? How corny can you get? I can't believe that you used that line and that she fell for it? I you sure you didn't tell her that the phone number was for your report?"

Rico smiles and shrugs sarcastically.

"What was I supposed to say?" asked John. "…and the rest was history?"

"It is history, now that you made me tell that story again, for the millionth time. Why are you busting my huevos?"

"How do you feel now?"

"Pretty good. I guess it *has* been an unusual relationship from the very beginning."

"You're in an unusual line of work and you do it a little differently than most."

"You can't do it *too* differently, though or you end up like Vito and no matter how you do it, well the people who love you are going to be scared." Both men grow noticeably quiet and solemn.

Johnny adds wisely, "You can imagine how Susie feels. People don't shoot or stab doctors or lawyers or even martial arts instructors that often, you know."

"You sound like my parents. They used to hide my homework when I went into the Academy. My father's never forgiven me...for not becoming *anything* but a cop."

"Maybe everyone's trying to tell you something?"

"Maybe...but maybe I'm just not able to listen. Maybe I'm not that smart, or too single-minded. Maybe I'm only good at offering advice to other people and can't take my own advice. Maybe that's what it takes to be a good cop."

"Maybe," Johnny conceded.

Chapter Five
Ls and Ws

The day of Vito's funeral was another beautiful day in Southern California. It just seemed wrong to Rico. Though the gravesite was silent, there was something odd about a procession and an occasional convertible with its top down. Rows upon rows of police cars, marked and unmarked and motorcycles sporting officers in full dress continued to arrive at the scene.

In the back seat of one limo, the car directly behind the hearse, Vito's wife, Rico and Susie sat together. Rico sat at one window, Susie at the other and Becky in the middle. Rico and Susie glanced uncomfortably at each other several times. This went unnoticed by Becky, who was sitting motionless, deep in mourning. As the hearse and this limo arrived there was a moment of jockeying for position so that the car holding the coffin could get close enough to unload the body.

Susie emerged first when the limo stopped and helped Becky exit the vehicle. Rico was last to depart as Becky took a few steps forward, away from Susie and Rico. All eyes were on her. It was as if no one wanted to even look at the hearse or coffin. Rico took Susie by the arm and whispered, "I need to talk to you a minute."

"What's there to talk about? This is not a good time."

"I have to help carry Vito's body. We have to be together for awhile. Let's try and, at least be friendly for Becky's sake."

In a leading tone, she responds, "Fine. Is there anything else?"

Seizing the opportunity quickly, Rico responds, "Yes. I still love you. I'd like to try and work it out later, if we can."

As Rico starts to move toward the coffin, Becky looks impatient. Both begin talking fast, showing some embarrassment, but wanting to make sure that the conversation continues before Rico must take his place as a pall-bearer. Vito's coffin has been pulled out of the hearse, on a giant shelf that is attached to the interior of the car.

"I'm sorry but today, here is not a good time to make a case for us. I don't feel like I'd win in a competition between me and your work... And I don't want to worry about what's happened to you when you're away from me. I don't want to come to another cop funeral."

Rico reaches out and takes Susie's hand briefly, then drops it and falls into place at the head, left corner of the casket. Susie returns the touch, but it is obvious to both that while they may love each other, and want to remain friends, a relationship is just too frightening for Susie.

After placing the coffin into position, Rico moves between the two women and takes both of their arms, leading them into a position at the center of attention. All three look around the area, seeing the same things but reacting differently. A rider-less horse, officers in full-dress uniforms, twenty-one gun salute, all have a very different impact on Becky, Susie and Rico. When they are in position, they stand a moment, a minister raises a book and speaks words that none of them hear.

The funeral is over. Almost all onlookers have departed. Rico, Susie and Becky are still in the same place. The casket is gone, out of sight. Some are saying their condolences to Becky; she is barely responding. Rico and Susie are discussing what they should do with Becky.

"Maybe we should stay with her today."

"You're the cop, the one with a life and death schedule to keep. Do you have the time?"

"The chief gave me a few days off. I can be with you two as long as I like."

Susie smiles and shakes her head affirmatively and moves a few steps toward Becky who is nearby. Chief Sheer steps up to Becky from the opposite side, to the rear of Rico so Rico is startled when Sheer speaks. "Pretty sad day, huh?"

Rico, turns and answers, trying to conceal his shock, "Uh, yes sir. It is."

"He was a good friend of yours wasn't he?"

"We were the best of friends, but more than that. He was my first partner."

"Yeah...You'll be happy to know then, that I've decided to let you poke around on this one, though I have to tell you there is not much in a official files that will be of help."

Rico lights up. His eyes widen, almost happily.

"You can work with your current partner. What's his name again?"

"Ron, sir. Ron Sullivan."

"Right. I also want you to be directly connected to Sergeant Vic Berman and to Detective John Williams."

Suspiciously, Rico responds "I appreciate your letting me work with Berman, sir. But, why Williams?"

"I don't really appreciate the cross-examination. To answer your question because he's heading homicide's end of things and because he's the best cop there is today. You got something against Williams? Of all people, I thought you'd and he would get along fine."

Rico, remembered meeting Williams at the station. A clean-cut, younger version of Rico, in uniform was holding a folder out to a cop behind a desk. "Could you just take a look at this to see if I filled it out properly?"

"Why don't you go show that to Detective Williams? He knows all about everything." The young officer pointed across the crowded office space, indicating Williams.

Rico walked over to Williams' desk. Williams tried to make himself look busy by moving his typewriter one inch in several directions and back again to the staring point. He then opened and closed all his desk drawers and checked the lead on his pencils as if they were the tips of arrows.

Not dissuaded, Rico broke the ice in a very friendly tone, "Hi. I'm Rico Rose."

Williams cut Rico off merely by looking up angrily. "I know who the hell you are. Didn't you just hear that guy? I know all about everything. What the fuck do I care who you are? I don't want to associate with a little dumb shit of a boot. What are you trying to do? Contaminate me?" Williams stood, opening and slamming shut one of the drawers once again and stormed away, leaving Rico dumbfounded.

"Well?" Sheer's voice shakes Rose from his vivid memory.

"It's not that, sir. It's just that I think he has something against me."

"That's nonsense. Williams hates everyone equally. Anyway, we're not choosing up sides for volleyball, Rose. This is your *team*. You're part of a police investigative *team* on this one. Take it or leave it."

Rico, thinking only briefly says, " I'll take it, sir. And, thank you."

Sheer waves off any thanks and walks away. Rico looks in the direction of Susie and Becky, still receiving well wishers. He glances around sizing up each and every face. He knows that often a killer will try to crash the funeral of his victim, and he does not want that to be the case here.

His attention is gathered by a small group of men who have huddled together and are just breaking up their conversation. Rico walks away from Becky and Susie and toward this group, speaking to one of them that he recognizes.

"Ron, we got the job."

"I know. The big chief dropped over to warn me. When do you want to slip out of these dress-blues and into something dirty and more comfortable? I'm ready now."

Rico hesitates, looks in the direction of Susie and Becky who are walking their way. Ron Sullivan reads the situation, understanding by the look on Rico's face.

"I'll go call Berman. He gets off duty in an hour. He'll probably want to meet with us right away." Rico nods and Ron exits as Becky and Susie walk up.

"You got the job, didn't you?" Becky was anxious to find the one who had killed her husband.

Susie looks frightened, confused and angry all at once. "What job?"

Ignoring Susie, Rico responds to Becky, "Yeah, I got it."

Becky speaks directly to Susie, "Rico's going to find Vito's killer."

Rico explains and apologizes at the same time, as he responds, "Ron and Vic wanted to get together, just for a little while... There on this with me."

Susie understands that her anger is unwarranted, but she cannot control herself. She remains silent.

Becky speaks directly again to Susie, coaxingly as if the two have discussed things privately. "It's Vito's killer. This is different. He has to go."

"Try to get back as soon as you can." Susie softens and tries not to overreact according to her old script. "I'm going to stay with Becky. You can find us at her place, if you need us."

Rico nods and takes Susie's hand once again. She smiles slightly and moves Becky off, toward the waiting car. Rico watches the two women leave and hears, noticing heavy footsteps from behind, that Ron is returning. "Berman says he'll be ready in half an hour."

Rico looks at Ron, near expressionless, waiting for more information. "He'll meet us at Hell Hole," Ron adds.

In a coffee shop, back over the hills and in the Valley, a blond haired man, about thirty, short and husky, is sitting at a booth. Rico and Ron enter and walk up to him. This is Berman.

"Where's your date?" Rico asks, as he and his partner sit.

Berman looks at Ron and responds, as if the question came from him. "Yours is kinda cute. Maybe I should try for him first, before you pollute him."

"Hey, I'm not a piece of meat! I have feelings! I'm a real person." Rico shouts, playing along. "Anyway, I'm taken, you asshole. You're paired up with Williams."

"Yeah, I heard he was in on this. That guy hates my guts."

"According to the Chief, he hates everyone," Ron announces knowingly. "He knows every bad ass on the streets, though."

"We don't have to actually work with him, I guess. But, Sheer said he's on the team or else there's no team."

Berman shrugs and shakes his head. "We don't have to actually work *with* anyone. But, we'd better be careful how we operate on this one."

"How so?" Ron wants to know.

"The talk around the department is that Vito might've been on the take."

"That's fucked up. It's crazy. I can guarantee Morelli!" Rico was not containing his anger very well right now. "Which is more than I can say for Williams, or you two assholes for that matter."

"Take it easy Rose. I'm only saying what I've heard."

"He was more honest than anyone," Rico continues. "That's probably the reason he's dead."

"You might not be too far wrong," Berman spoke cryptically, as if he knew something he was not saying.

Sullivan jumped right on it. "O.K. What the fuck's *that* supposed to mean?"

"It means that there's a big I.A. rump-roast going on and there has been for about two months now. Vito might have found out about something more than just dope, more than he was looking for. You know how he was. He just kept following the trial like a hungry wolf and it made some people very nervous."

"You think that's why he was wasted?" Rico had yet to respond, but was paying close attention.

"Either that, or as usual, the money was talking. Some big money guys were probably starting to feel squeezed. In any case, the word is to be *extremely* careful how we handle this. Everything by the book. When we find Vito's killer, we don't want anything to screw it up."

"Sure Sarge. Just like always."

"No, not just like always. If there's anything out of the ordinary about how this little team operates, we'll all find ourselves with transfers to little known, out-of-the way places where barking dogs are the big crime."

"You mean more out of the fucking way than San Fernando?" All three laugh.

"Did homicide come up with anything?" In a very businesslike manner, Rico guides the conversation.

Berman takes Rico's change of demeanor in stride, "The guy or guys who did him, were experts with a knife."

"So are half the hoods on the street," Sullivan speaks softly, as if to himself as much as anyone.

"Well, this guy was so good that they couldn't decide if one man could have hit so many vital organs in such a short span of time, or if there was more than one knife."

"Was it more than one?" Rico was still in detective mode.

"Sure," adds Sullivan. "One guy couldn't have taken Vito that easily, not without a fight."

"The thing is," Berman speaks to no one in particular. "The odds of more than one guy having that kind of skill and being in the same place at the same time, is pretty unlikely. It would be like two surgeons had become criminals. And, they would have had to be using the same kind of blade, something unusual according to the Coroner. I'm not sure if there was any extensive forensics done, but we know that he was clean. They always check for drugs in cops first. I figure Vito was trying to do a solo act, trying to make a buy to lead him to the big guy or something like that, and he got made. Sometimes cops just get overanxious and careless."

The other two men are silent. They agree but don't want to admit it.

"So, where does that leave us? Where do we start?" Rico also speaks to no one, but is voicing a general question.

"There isn't anything else we can do until we hit the streets...Are you two guys heading out now?"

"Not yet," Rico looks directly at Ron when he answers, even though he is responding to Berman's question. "I've got a promise to keep."

Later, Ron Sullivan and Rico Rose are in a car; Ron is driving.

"Turn here," Rico points, giving directions and waits for car to complete its turn. Now just head straight for about..." Rico's voice trails off as he sees something of interest. "Make a U and follow that Chevy."

Ron does not question the change of direction, but simply makes appropriate motions as soon as safely possible. "What the hell are we turning around for?"

"Did you see that carload of Cholos? We're gonna take 'em.

"Why? We're not even officially on duty!"

"Cause their license told me they got that car in Crenshaw."

"Oh, out-of-towners here for the gang-bangers convention, huh?"

"They've got no business being around here. They're here to do somebody." Rico lifts a light and waves the Chevy to side of road as he and Ron pull alongside.

There is no chase. The Chevy just pulls over slowly and comes to a stop. Rico and Ron exit their vehicle and advance on the gang members from opposite sides of their vehicle. Rico has his shotgun propped against his hip. He points it into the open rear passenger window of the car and makes his commands. "O.K. vatos, one shot from this and you're all taken care of. Do exactly as I tell you. Get out of the car and keep your hands where we can see them."

There are five young men, two in front and three in back.

The youths exit and are directed to lie prone, face down on the concrete in a semi-circle around Officer Sullivan's feet. Silent crowd control is achieved with head-bobs and waves of the shotgun muzzle. Rico then hands Ron the shotgun, who holsters his own weapon and keeps the shotgun pointed at the youths. With their heads at his feet it is easy keep an eye on the whole group and if one looks up, they will be staring up the barrel of a shotgun.

Rico does the honors of searching the boys. He gets to the last one and signals with a shake of his head to Ron that he's found nothing. Ron signals him, also non-verbally, toward the car and steps back, still pointing the shotgun.

"Alright, everybody stand up."

They stand.

"Now, one at a time I'm going to ask you who you are. I want your real names and then I want your street names. Your real names don't mean nada to me."

Rico steps up close to the first youth in line.

"What's your name?"

"George Martinez."

Impatiently Rico growls, "What's your *street name*, pendejo?"

The boy stares stupidly as Ron walks over and threatens to hit youth with the butt of the gun. The boy stumbles back, and the others get restless, but Ron drops the barrel of the gun, back toward the youths and they fall back into line.

Angrily, Rico continues, "Cut the crap. I ain't your mama. Now, what's your street name?"

"Loco."

Ron hands the shotgun back to Rico and goes into the Chevy. Rico glances towards the car. Ron searches for a moment, but finds nothing. He signals to Rico, again frantically.

Rico, unperturbed moves onto next boy in line. "What's your name?"

"Fernando Martin. I don't have a street name, ala brava man."

Immediately Ron walks over threatening with his redrawn sidearm, and then drags Fernando over to the sidewalk, away from the group.

Ron is tugging at the boy's shirt until he rips one sleeve off which reveals a tattoo on the boy's shoulder. The words: "The Duke" are written in ink. Ron signals Rico.

"You want to be little jerks?' He looks to others in the group. My partner here will practice butt strokes across your empty heads if that's the game you want to play."

Rico goes over to the boy on the concrete and looks at the tattoos.

"You're *The Duke*, your majesty," state Rico emphatically.

Ron addresses the rest of the boys, "Anyone else feel their mind clearing up?" He taps the gun with his free hand.

The three remaining boys speak at once, "I'm Roco. Pepe. I'm Sleepy-dog."

Rico realizing a further search is without merit. "O K vatos listen up. This isn't your barrio. I don't know who you were coming here to dust, or how you were planning to do it with only your dicks in your hands, but you better split and don't ever come back to this side of the city again."

Rico and Ron back slowly to their car and they depart. The boys do the same. Rico has gotten to the driver's side, somehow and therefore is driving now.

After the car is underway, Ron breathes a heavy sigh.

"What the hell, Rico. Not even a joint. No guns, not even a seed, nothing. We can get indicted for pulling stuff like that. Good thing, those little shits don't know their rights."

Rico is steaming mad, "I don't get it. I know they're assholes. I can feel it. *They* know they're not supposed to be around here. I know they're trying to blow somebody away. Don't worry; they aren't going to say anything to anyone. Believe me."

Ron is not dropping the subject. "Not anything. There weren't any guns. How could they kill somebody? There wasn't anything."

Rico, extremely angry decides to turn the car back around.

"God damn it."

"What the hell are you doing?"

After driving only a few seconds Rico points. "Fucking Hell! Look at that." He points with a glance to the side of the road.

"There's another one. There's *six* now." The Chevy is parked on the opposite side of the four-lane road.

"They must have picked him up just now," Ron realizes aloud.

"After dropping him off when they saw us turn around the first time." Rico stops the car and two cops jump out advancing quickly and yelling new commands for the group to get out of their Chevy and "assume the position."

The group quickly drops to the sidewalk with their palms flat on the concrete.

Rico begins searching the new youth first this time and Ron is again holding the shotgun. Rico pulls a 45 automatic from the young man's waist band, shows it to Ron. Both cops smile. Just then, over the radio they hear... *"All units, be on the look out for a carload of youths in a blue, Chevrolet sedan. There are six youths; one is armed with a forty-five caliber automatic pistol. They are wanted in regards to a murder and are considered dangerous."*

Rico walks over to the radio while the above is still in the process of being said. He gets to the radio at the end of the comment and takes the microphone to his lips to speak.

"This is officer Rose. We already have the suspects in custody.

"Rico, is that you?"

"Yeah, Tom it's me. I have the suspects right here...the shooter and the gun. Who got popped? Was it a celebrity?"

"Does it really matter?" came the response.

Chapter Six
What's in a name?

Paloma is nonchalant and relaxed as he faces two men in suits.

"Why the fuck did you kill a cop? Don't you realize that we don't need this shit right now? We're sitting on a huge nest egg."

"Yeah, a golden egg!" Another suit shouts proudly, as if making a brilliant literary reference. "…That we need to cut and move before it spoils. Our investors want to stay low profile and then you go and kill a fucking cop!"

"I didn't know it was a cop!" Paloma was lying.

"And, I suppose you didn't know that he was The Panda's old partner?"

"I don't give a damn about no Teddy Bear and where does it say you can't kill a cop. He was just a junkie! I knew there was something wrong and I took care of it."

"No. He was playin' you bro. He was no junkie and you didn't take care of nothing. You fucked up big time!"

"Don't worry. I'm the best asset you have and I move more shit than all of your other pushers combined."

"We're not saying you're not a good worker, a true friend of the la familia, but these new shipments are making us all worry."

"I told you I will personally handle the shipments. It's obvious, just like always, if I want something done right, I'll have to do it myself!"

There was no subtlety in Paloma's statement. He wanted to them all to know that only *he* was brave enough and skillful enough to kill a cop and get away with it.

Also, showing contempt for La Familia would not have been a good idea for anyone else, but the one known as Paloma had made a name for himself as being above even the code of the street. No one was quite sure how he'd attained this status. It just seemed like suddenly, he'd appeared on the scene and was somehow a shot-caller with connections that went all the way back to the joint and to La Familia's Mexican roots.

Paloma's birth name was Fernando Inez, but no one in the abandoned warehouse where the meeting is taking place know anything about his ancient past. This is mostly the result of careful planning and abject paranoia on Paloma's part.

A few locals can trace the legends back as far as one other alias, but here, no one knows Paloma for who is truly is, a scared bully who uses bravado to mask his own terror. Fernando was born in El Paso, Texas to two legal immigrants. His mother cleaned houses and took care of other people's children. His father was a gardener who wanted nothing but the best for his family. Fernando was the youngest of three sons. His oldest brother worked with Fernando's father while the second brother had disappeared back to Mexico before Fernando could remember. *Nando*, as his mother called him, never had a very good opinion of himself. He struggled in school and was awkward in social situations. It wasn't that he didn't have advantages or intelligence. His parents took very good care of him and his teachers said that he was *'smart but just didn't apply himself.'* It was just that Fernando was embarrassed by who he was. He was embarrassed by his upbringing, by the jobs that his parents did and by the fact that they were from Mexico. He vowed never to become a servant like either one of his parents, even though many of their clients were also immigrants.

Nando's mother was much more accepting of her youngest's moodiness, but his father had a tendency to give only one chance to each child to fail or succeed. If they did not chose to succeed, to the best of their ability, then the father wrote them off. Of his son, Fernando he was heard to say, "Some people are just bad. There is no reason to make bones for a jelly-fish."

This suited Nando just fine. He had no intentions of staying in this family any longer than suited his selfish interests. When the second oldest disappeared, this gave Fernando a chance to slip even further below the radar and his mother a pat excuse for ignoring Nando's shortcomings. When a neighbor's dog or cat ended up mutilated or poisoned, after coincidentally having a run in with Nando, the mother would only comment on how sad Rudy was that his brother had left him. This went on for seventeen year, until Fernando Inez left Texas in his dust.

Becky's house is a total wreck. Tables are turned over, drawers are opened, the contents dumped. Becky and Susie are sitting on a couch at the center of the mess. There is a large bottle of wine, almost empty sitting on a coffee table in front of them. They both hold glasses and are obviously drunk. Both women are talking in an extremely, slurred speech.

"I don't think I could handle it the way you are," said Susie.

"I'm not handling anything that I haven't handled a hundred times before." Becky as if singing adds, "It's second nature to me now…I've thought about Vito's death so many times…I've lived it in my mind…When it finally happened, I was already used to it."

"Why do they do it? Why do they love it so?"

"They're not people…not people like the rest of us." Susie looks at her as if she is insane.

"What did you say?" Susie said.

"They're a kind of breed, not people like us. Normal people don't like the idea that everything they do may be the last thing that they EVER do." Reflecting, she continues, "I don't think they could understand how we feel, but if they DID understand, then we wouldn't love them so much. Then they'd be just like the rest of us. They wouldn't be cops."

Susie responds after long deliberation. "That's really crazy."

Becky nods her agreement and there is a knock at the door. Neither woman moves to answer. The door opens and Rico enters. He slowly lets himself in and stands at the doorway, amazed at the mess.

"What the hell happened here?" he wants to know.

Becky answers, giggling, "The place's been ransacked! Quick call the cops."

Susie chimes in, "Look, they've arrived already."

Rico walks over, stumbling on the mess a few times,

"You...you're drunk!"

"You see what a good detective he is?" Becky speaks to Susie with a disgusted smirk on her face. Both laugh and clarify, in turn by adding, "We found it this way when we got here..."

"...We found the door open too."

"We decided to wait." Becky holds up a glass, as if explaining. "...until you got here to decide what to do. We didn't know you were going to be this long."

Rico goes directly to telephone and dials. "Hi, Tom? This is Rico again. Yeah, listen, Becky's place's been searched...No, I don't think anything was taken. It looks like a professional job." Rico looks over at women as if thinking. "No...on second thought, I don't think there was any damage at all. Maybe you could just send someone out tomorrow to take a report...Right, she doesn't need anything else today." Hanging up the phone, Rico looks at the two women and shakes his head, unbelieving. "Let's get you two into bed."

"Oh, good," Susie says, without realizing her double entendre.

Rico quietly closes a side door of the house, as if someone on the other side is sleeping and walks to the telephone again. He dials with purpose.

In a small apartment Ron is at home, relaxing in a chair. His phone rings. Answering, he says, "Yeah? Hey, Panda. I thought you were going to be tied up...You bet I'll pick you up, first thing in the morning. He hangs up and sinks back into his chair.

The next morning Rico comes out of his house to Ron, who is waiting in a gray sedan. Rico gets into the car and the two drive away. Rico speaks the first words between the two.

"Where're we heading first?"

"I thought we could try the most notorious hot bed of corruption and crime..."

Rico interrupts, "This week, you must mean...Brand Park?"

Ron nods, which Rico sees from the corner of his eye as Ron continues. "We haven't been around for a couple of days, maybe everyone will think we've retired...the place will probably be jumping."

After a short drive, the two super cops are pulling into the parking lot of a small park. The unmarked car drives along the perimeter of the lot for a few seconds, slowly, and then stops next to a group of three obvious narcotics users. The three young men are trying to act invisible. The camera angle adjusts to show the passenger side of the car. Rico rolls down the window, recognizing one of the men.

"Conejo. Que Paso?"

"Panda, Mi carnal. Where have you been? I missed you."

"Conejo? Is that you? You look terrible. Have you been chipping again?" Rico opens the passenger door and gets out.

"No, ala brava, es'ay."

Rico takes both of Conejo's arms by the wrists and turns the forearms upward. While he begins to examine Conejo for injection marks, Roy also steps out of car and walks over, keeping the other men and Rico in front of him.

"I don't know. That could be a mark; that looks like one," Rico comments casually, which seems to send Conejo into a smiling, yet frightened response.

"I've always been straight with you Panda. I just gave blood, I swear.

Rico looks at and speaks to Ron, who continues watching the other men. "I think we've got a marks beef here. What do you think?" Ron shrugs, but does not look down or away from the group.

Conejo's fears continue to climb, "Hey, Panda, come on man. Those aren't marks. You know I've always been straight with you. I know what you're after. I've been listening--we all have. If we hear anything, we'll cut you in. I swear, we've always been straight with each other."

Rico continues to look at Ron, "I'd like to believe him. Really, I would. As far as I know, he has always been straight with me."

Ron's stare has become sinister. "I don't know the asshole. Maybe, if we shot his fucking head off and then ask one of these other fucks…" Ron suddenly lifts a shotgun from behind his back and points it at Conejo's chin.

Conejo's tone turns to one of pleading, "I don't want to look like a snitch."

Another young man in the group seems to break, "Tell them what we heard. It won't hurt to tell them what we heard."

Ron swings the barrel of the gun around and Rico turns back, keeping his eyes pinned on Conejo. "What did you hear?"

"It's just a name, ala brava."

"What name?"

"Just tell him, before we all go down!" A third youngster chimes in, trying to convince Conejo that he should talk.

"Paloma! Paloma! Some dude they call Paloma knows what happened to your friend. that's all we heard. Find Paloma and you'll find out what happened.

Ron drops the barrel of the gun and Rico lets go of Conejo's arms. The two cops look at each other and tilt their heads to signal that they are satisfied.

Rico speaks casually to Conejo. "O.K. Bro. We're up and up." Then, his tone chills. "But the next time I have to ask a question twice, you go to jail."

The two cops get into their car. Rico leans out the window and says , as if giving everyday advice, "You better start drying out quick Conejo...you stay loaded and there's not going to be any more favors." Then turning to the boy who was the first to break, he adds, "And if you hear anything else, you better let me know. I'm in a bad mood right now and I don't have much patience for this shit. I don't ordinarily go off on people, just because they are assholes, but I'm about to make an exception. Comprende?" He rolls up the window and the car begins to move.

As the car moves out of ear-shot, Ron asks, "What do you think?"

"I think we should find out who the *pigeon* is."

"The pigeon?"

"Yeah, Paloma means pigeon in Spanish my monolingual partner." Suddenly Rico spots something and points, "Look, it's Ace Jenkins. What the fuck? He's dirty too!"

"How can you tell from here? He's not doing anything."

"Let's not waste time on details. I can tell. Let's take him and find out where all the shit is flooding in from."

Immediately Ron screeches to a halt and the two cops jump out.

Ace Jenkins is a slow to react, middle aged, black man, wearing a long trench coat.

He is trying to look inconspicuous as he ignores the screeching tires, and continues walking past the officers at a quick pace. His coat makes him particularly obvious. As Rico and Ron approach, there is a moment of indecision. Then suddenly Ace begins to run at top speed his coat, trailing behind him, but his hands still in his pockets. Ron and Rico also begin to run. Abruptly, Rico stops shakes his head as if he cannot believe what he's doing, takes out his handgun and points it in the direction of the running suspect.

"I'll kill you, Ace. I'm don't like to run and I'm not a good enough shot to try and wound you."

The man stops running. All are breathing hard. Ron moves up from behind and takes Ace down hard. He lies face down with his arms and legs spread. Ron immediately begins to search pulling out several weapons, knives, handguns, one after another. He pulls Ace up abruptly as Rico comes from behind and puts an arm-bar to Ace's throat.

"Do you want to go down again? How many strikes you got already?"

Coughing, Ace mutters, "Why do you have a hard-on for me?"

Rico applies more pressure. "Cause, you're an asshole. Hawking guns is illegal, Ace. I don't mind if gang-bangers kill each other, but that's not what happens. Your smuggled goods have killed a cop and probably a punch of innocent little kids. If you don't want to get stepped on, then you better start singing."

"I (choke) ain't talking (choke) *here*."

Ron slides between the two men and takes charge of Ace.

They put handcuffs on him and begin walking toward the car. Rico is a few paces ahead.

Ron speaks to Ace in a friendly tone, "The Panda's not a bad cop. He just doesn't like to be bull-shitted. When he gets mad, well, sometimes I can hardly stop him. He's in a bad mood right now. His friend got blown away...his old partner." He pushes Ace's head into the car.

"The words out," Ace begins to speak, knowingly as soon as he's safely inside the car. What do you think I am, the guy who did it? I don't use much. I just do burgs and fence stolen property."

Ron pushes Ace inside the car and follows him into back seat.

"We know that. Rico knows that too. We only want to put the pushers in the joint.

"Oh, yeah? I just saw you two let three vatos go free, because they were willing to help out. Those muthafuckers are dead."

"What'd you mean by that? What did they die of?" Rico wanted to know.

"They're zombies. They're bought and paid for. Their tickets are punched. Anyone seen talking to you two who doesn't go to jail is dead meat, that's what I mean. The car begins to move with Rico at the wheel. Both Rico and Ron are silent, they are thinking. Ace is looking them over and breaks the silence.

"With all your super-powers, don't you get it? That's why I let you two turkeys chase after me. I *wanted* to talk." Ace puffs out his chest proudly. "But, I ain't no young fool though. I'm a *veterano*. I'm going to be around a lot longer. Those three are dead.

"Who says they're dead?" Ron took over the questioning now, with rapid-fire precision. Ace's answers come just as quickly.

"Ain't sure, but it's a big voice. There's a lot of bread involved...A LOT of bread."

"What's the money buying?"

"What's the smart money, the big money usually buy? What is there a lot of on the street right now?"

"Dope?"

"That's the *boy*." Ace puts emphasis on last word as it is slang for heroin. Rico interjects.

"Heroin!"

"You win the prize, Panda. Now, guess the color."

Ron answers this one, resuming his questioning. "Brown?"

"Right again," Ace responds. "You're both bright cops!"

Ron speaks to himself, as much as he does to Rico. "Chicano mafia..."

Rico grows quickly anxious and blurts out, "We need names and numbers!"

"I don't know the whole itinerary, but here's the end of my lullaby...I'm not much of a doper, but this stuff on the street is pure bunk. Everybody's got their savior. Every gutter has its lead rat. One lone rat has been very busy lately."

Rico interrupts, "Who was the mother fucker, who needed to kill a cop?"

"The word is he didn't need to kill him, not for a little junk-dealer bust. The word is it was a set up, because your friend was getting too close to the big boys and some secrets that nobody was supposed to hear." Ace pauses for effect. "The word on my side of town...is that a *little bird* did it just for fun."

Rico and Ron realize and speak simultaneously, "Paloma!"

Then Ron calls from the backseat.

"What should we do with your friend here?"

Rico speaks to Ace. "Do you want us to let you out someplace?"

Ace just shakes his head in disbelief. "Hell no! Ain't you been listening? I want you two turkeys to haul my ass to jail and book me. You know I'm high. I'll show you the marks if you need evidence." There's another pause, but this time for confusion. "Don't you guys listen? I haven't told you *nothing*. Get it? Don't do me any favors that are going to get me killed. Just *book* me, and remember, I ain't told you *nothin'*."

Rico and Ron pull up in front of a small flower shop in the business district. The car screeches to a halt and both men are seen to laugh, inside. Rico jumps out, speaks a few words through the open door. The words aren't heard as they are drown out by traffic noise, but the source of the humor seems to have something to do with the way Rico is driving. Ron stays in the car but doesn't leave. Rico goes inside.

Inside the shop Rico finds Susie behind the counter. He moves in swiftly and she is working, slouched over counter. She doesn't immediately see him.

"Hi, Hon. How's your head?" he asks when he is directly in front of her.

"Oh!" Startled, she looks up. "I don't know. I'm too busy thinking about how bad my stomach feels to think about my head. Listen, maybe we should take being just friends more seriously. Please don't call me *Hon*. Okay?"

"Okay, Susie. But, why don't you see if you can go home early? You can leave now and I'll have Ron drop you off."

"It's only a couple more hours. Anyway, if I go home now, The Old Bag…" Susie indicates over her shoulder with a glance. "…will know I'm hung-over."

Rico laughs. "O.K. Hhh...Susie. I'll see you later. I just wanted to see how you were doing."

Susie leans across counter to kiss Rico instinctively, but then pulls back, realizing that this is a breach of the new relationship and says, "Thanks." She smiles then frowns as if sick to her stomach.

"I hope it wasn't just the thought of kissing me that made you look like that," Rico jokes, exits, and returns to the car.

Chapter Seven
Tears for Rudolfo Montillo

A black-and-white police car is seen parking near a group of three, male individuals. One of the men is the murderer Paloma. There are two others, both grizzly looking Chicanos. The squad car parks and Irish and Rainbow get out. They walk slowly over to the group. The group is sitting on and around an old car. The three men are unconcerned about the advancing cops.

"Montillo, anything happening?" Polonowski speaks to Paloma, who he knows by another name, Rudolfo Montillo.

"Rainbow, how's it? Catch any bad boys lately?" The other two men laugh curiously.

Big John continues, "We're looking for info. Got any news about what happened the other day?"

"What makes you think I know what's going on? I'm stupid."

Irish interjects sarcastically, "I'm not going to argue with you about that, but we heard you were like the priest here and we were hoping you were willing to break your vows of silence, Montillo. We wanted to be around when it happened."

All laugh then Rainbow continues resignedly, "This was just a friendly visit. We can see from your face that you've done a bullet, so you can preach to this choir from a place of knowledge. I just thought I smelled ether, like the odor on you lips and hands."

"You thought we was smoking Sherms? You know we don't do that sort of thing. Those drugs can *kill* you." Montillo/Paloma's two cohorts laugh so hard that one begins to cough.

McCoy looks him over and comments to Montillo, "Maybe your friend could use a sermon on the evils of smoking, padre."

Montillo smiles and starts to make the sign of the cross, tangling it up and turning it into a pentagram. The cops think nothing of it and begin to walk away.

Then Rainbow turns back and says, "Well, you boys let us know if you hear anything...O.K.?"

"You betcha, officers!" Montillo speaks with a geek-inflection, salutes as the two uniforms return to their vehicle and depart. Montillo is wearing a sleeveless shirt, but he's been facing the two cops the whole conversation. If they had seen him from behind they would have noticed that on his left shoulder, not visible from the from is a crude tattoo of a bird, although a single tear tattooed on Montillo's face, is clearly visible just below his left eye.

Montillo's face changes from a friendly smile to hate as the cops drive off.

"Fucking bastards."

In the car, Polonowski makes this pronouncement, "That guy is the lowest piece of shit."

The three men on the street begin to move away from one another, making hand gestures and signing club affiliations. Montillo gets into a gray sedan and starts the engine. Once he is alone his face goes blank and he shivers with fear.

Montillo drives a short distance, stops and looks at a group of very young Chicano kids, smoking marijuana cigarettes.

He has rounded a corner just next to them, so that what they are doing is obvious. Also it is obvious that he is looking at them and is affected by what he sees. There is a chain link fence along the street where he's stopped the car. He is really shaken now.

He stares at the fence and three names begin to echo in his head. Each name is sounded separately then overlapped with the other two. The names are (in this order) MONTILLO/PALOMA/FERNANDO INEZ. As he stares at the fence and the names echo he begins to drift back into his memories. Perhaps the chain link fence and the surreptitious actions of the youth have combined to recall a familiar scene. When Paloma was Fernando Inez, he had his first stay in prison. The streets of the city reminded him of the prison yard.

Montillo can see himself standing at a chain link fence. He is a younger version of himself. He is staring blankly, sadly through the fence. There are a number of inmates walking around behind Montillo. Another Chicano walks up behind him, unseen. The man who comes up is about thirty-five. He is strong and mean looking. His face is tattooed with several tears under his left eye. Because of the torrent of fake tears, this man is known as Lloron, Spanish for Crybaby.

He is the first to speak to Paloma, "Your name's Fernando Inez?

"Yes. How did you know?"

"I know everything around here, compadre." He glances back and forth like an animal on the prowl, and then continues.

"They call me Lloron." He points to his tattoos and Fernando nods his understanding.

"You're here because you like to smoke."

"I got popped for weed. It was bogus but a year can go by quickly."

"Or a year can be a bullet to life. It may *never* end." Lloron lets his ominous statement sink in, meaning that people often get caught up in the system, struggling to survive while doing a short amount of time. They end up committing more and more serious crimes, until they are either killed or end up serving life sentences.

"Have you been approached yet?"

"Approached? By who?"

"By anyone. There are many choices and many dangers here, especially if you are alone. Some men will try to use you like a *chauala*. Some will try to use you in other ways." Fernando's eyes widen imperceptibly as Lloron continues. "I could help you."

"You aren't alone?"

Lloron lifts his shirt slightly, revealing a finely crafted, homemade knife. "I'm not alone when I carry this. Everyone knows I am the I best with one of these," he adds proudly. "I'm feared by the others and so are my friends."

"What does one have to do to become your friend?" Fernando asks suspiciously.

"Not anything in particular." He smiles. "There might be a little favor. I may ask that you get me something or give me some of your food when I'm hungry, nothing you wouldn't mind doing for a friend."

Fernando looks over his shoulder at the inmates. The camera pans the yard. There is nothing but bad looking people walking there. The "new fish" Fernando is truly frightened. He looks resignedly back at Lloron who smiles, reaches out and shakes Fernando's hand.

Later, on a walkway between two rows of cells, a voice calls from one cell to another next door. The voice is Lloron's.

"Fernando?"

"Yes."

"Did you get your fahos today?"

"Yes."

"I want them."

Fernando drops his head, dejectedly but in the shadows he is unseen. "Yes." Fernando's hand and arm reach around the bars from one cell to the other as he hands Lloron his cigarettes.

On another day, the prisoners are all sitting around long, large metal tables talking in low tones and eating chow. Fernando and Lloron are sitting at one table. Fernando looks morose. Lloron is talking and pointing with his gaze, as he speaks. "The leader of the *miates* (he says this with a Spanish accent) is that bald headed one. His name is Death. He hates Chicanos, so stay away from him when I'm not there. That one, the veterano, is Italiano. They think they own us all. Not in here they don't, but he does own many. Watch out for him. The Italianos still are very powerful." Lloron looks down at the food on Fernando's plate, "Do you want those?" He scrapes the food into his own plate, then continues as Fernando looks defeated. "The most dangerous is that fat old Mexicano."

Fernando looks up, curious about this latest bit of information. "The Chicano? Why, him?"

"He's the Mexican Mafia leader, but most of all he's my enemy." Lloron measures his words. "And now he is your enemy as well."

Fernando's face sags even further.

Lloron punctuates the lesson with a final comment, "I was very cold last night. I'll need to get one of your blankets before tonight."

The next day, in the yard Fernando and Lloron are sitting together. Lloron is merely sunning himself. His eyes are closed. Fernando looks anxiously around, twitching at every new approach or sound. He turns as if to speak to Lloron, changes his mind then turns toward him again.

"Lloron?" Fernando's protector doesn't stir. "I think I should to learn to use a knife."

Lloron opens one eye. "You don't need to learn. Why would you want to? If you have a skill then there's always going to be somebody wanting to challenge you."

"I've been thinking about it. I'm only safe when I'm with you. And, you could be twice as safe if you had me with you and I could protect myself. I could also watch your back."

"How could I trust you?"

Fernando flinches as if hurt. "You are my carnal, mi amigo. You wouldn't have to teach me all that you know, only enough to protect myself when I'm alone."

"It's not an easy request. It's difficult to even get a blade; perhaps your desire isn't strong enough. Perhaps your enemies aren't real. Maybe you'd cut yourself by accident!" Lloron laughs at his own joke.

Fernando persists, with purpose and meaning. "My enemies are your own."

"I'll think about it," Lloron says and closes his eyes.

Lloron and Fernando are just sitting down to an afternoon meal and Fernando breeches the silence. "Have you thought about it?"

Looking at Fernando penetratingly. "Yes. I've decided to teach you."

Fernando smiles then tries to conceal his glee. "When can we begin?"

"Tomorrow."

The next day, in the yard Lloron and Fernando come from opposite directions and sit on the same bench.

Immediately, Fernando begins to speak. "Do you have the knife? Can we begin?"

"We can begin, but you won't be getting a blade until you're ready and the time is right."

"When will that be?"

"When you know what you need to know; When we don't need to practice anymore. Now we can't get caught using knives. We're just two amigos playing tag. I'll show you."

Here he faces Fernando as if he is ready to fight. He holds his hand *as if* he has a knife. Fernando rises slowly, a little confused, and he looks around the yard.

"Don't worry. The guards won't care if we play a little." Lloron points to his knife hand. "See, I don't have a blade. I'm just playing."

Understanding, Fernando gets into a ready position. "What should I do?"

"Come at me as if you want to hurt me. Try and hit me with your thumb."

After a moment's hesitation Fernando closes his fist, as if holding a knife handle and lunges. Immediately, he is swept off his feet by the rear leg of Lloron. Lloron quickly strikes Fernando several times, as if he's stabbing many areas. Fernando looks dazed as he is helped to his feet by Lloron.

"There's two lessons in one. Never do what your opponent wants you to do. And, the most important lesson: kill your enemy several times. Strike as many vital areas as you can. Once is never enough. Every enemy who is shown mercy and left alive, will come back to haunt you."

Over the course of the next few months, Fernando gains competence in the art of knife fighting, right under the noses of the guards, who allow this kind of interaction as long as it does not appear to spark real violence. One day, Fernando is deemed ready for the next step

"You've learned well," Lloron tells him after one of their sessions. I think you're now ready for the real thing."

"A blade?"

"Si. That too. Remember, I told you that obtaining a blade in here was difficult, but not impossible. There are three basic parts. The first is the creation of the blade."

At this point Lloron takes Fernando on an educational journey that begins in the prison gardening shop. A blade of an old lawn mower has been broken from the rusting machine and transferred by Lloron's *friends*, to the machine shop.

A burly looking fellow is grinding an automobile part on a wheel. He lifts his gaze and makes sure that he's not being watched then pulls out the mower blade, that has been crudely refined and shaped to resemble a knife, and begins to grind.

In the wood shop, the handle is being constructed. Two pieces of wood are being carved by separate inmates. When they are finished, one hands his section to the other and he fits them together.

In another machine shop two small studs are being made. They will lock the handle together over the blade. No two hands ever hold all the pieces. If one piece is detected, another replacement is already being made. Knives of superior quality and sharpness can be made from many substances, but steel is still preferred.

Later, in the yard Lloron receives the several parts of the knife, one by one. He puts the pieces together by sense of touch in plain view, as he works under cover of his clothing. It appears to the guards that he may be pleasuring himself, but since he's in plain sight, they do not confront him. The assembly of the blade is the most dangerous time.

When he is finished, Lloron passes the blade to Fernando during one of their "play" sessions.

Lloron pats Fernando on the back as yard time ends and they begin to move back, into their cells. "We can no longer practice in the yard. "

Fernando looks at him with a "but how?" expression.

"The lessons will be much shorter now, and much more difficult. Meet me at the shower, on the way to lock-up."

Lloron falls into line, just ahead of Fernando. Fernando watches Lloron leave. He reaches into his pocket and feels the knife and smiles.

Later, in the shower room there is a similar scene as before. Fernando now tries the moves he's learned, but now he holds the blade. Lloron corrects him briefly on how he holds the knife. "Never let any part of your weapons face your opponent, except for a killing part."

Lloron is just rising from the table where he and Fernando sit. He rises, leaving Fernando alone. In less than one year, Fernando has gained confidence and status with the other inmates. He no longer appears edgy, nervous or an "easy mark." When Lloron leaves, another inmate watches carefully. This is *Dreamer* the leader of the Mexican Mafia. Dreamer signals a man next to him to go over to Fernando when he is left alone. The man rises and walks past Fernando; he stops only briefly to relay a message.

"Dreamer wants to talk. The locker room, right after dinner." The messenger walks away and Fernando doesn't look up. It is obvious that he's seen and heard him, though.

Fernando walks into the locker room and Dreamer, with several of his men, is there. Fernando stops at the door briefly, examines the group and then enters.

"You wanted to see me?"

"I need your help."

"How can *I* help *you*?"

"There are some men, friends of mine on the outside, who don't want Lloron...to finish his time here. Are you willing to help? Or would you rather stay his slave forever?"

"I'll be out of here soon."

"But, your debt to Lloron will never be paid. His reach is long."

"What do you want me to do?"

"All you have to do is tell us when Lloron is unarmed, or make sure that he is. I don't care how you do it, I just don't want him to have his protection with him and I want to know when that is. I understand that you may also be protected now. I'll need to be assured that your blade won't come to his defense."

"What are you going to do to him?"

"We're going to make sure he never leaves this place. Are you willing to help?"

"How will this benefit me? Lloron is my friend. He takes care of me. If it were known that I turned on my friends, no one would trust me. Maybe *his* friends would kill me."

Dryly, Dreamer responds, "If you don't want to be my friend, then you will suffer the same fate as The Cryer. I know you are armed now. I know you have learned to use a knife. But, someday, sometime, inside or out you will be vulnerable. My reach is greater than Lloron's, especially on the outside. It only takes a moment to die."

Leaning in close so that no one but Dreamer can hear, "No one must know it was me."

"All you have to do is signal me. Me alone. I'll do the rest." Then, he adds with emphasis. My friends...*I* will owe *you* a great debt after that."

"Alright."

Three days later, Fernando and Lloron are sitting together in the yard and Fernando breaks the silence. "I'd like to work some more with real blades."

"We could work here. We have more time before we go inside."

"No. I need to work with my knife. Let's go inside now and work for a few minutes before lock-up."

"Well. I would, but I was afraid we might have a search. I'm not carrying right now."

"Maybe tomorrow then." Fernando rises. "I guess I'll go and work on my own." Fernando walks away from Lloron, trying not to reveal his sadness, confusion, or any other emotion in his face.

A swarm of inmates are beating someone in the hallway. There is a rush of violent action and then they back away and continue moving toward their respective cells as if nothing has happened, before guards are able to respond. Lloron's body is lying on the floor. He's dead.

Fernando sits alone now. A man walks up behind him and speaks to him from behind. "We don't like stool pigeons, and those who turn on our friends are our enemies."

Fernando rises to face the man. "What do you mean by that Juedo?"

"I mean what I said. Somebody set up Lloron. The Paloma who did it, is as good as dead."

Fernando reaches into his pocket. "Don't try to put the finger on me. My touch is deadly."

Juedo leans back slightly, unintentionally showing fear. "No one knows who it was...for sure. Some think that you may have had something to do with it, that's all."

"If you can prove anything then try and kill me. If not, then leave me alone."

Juedo begins to leave then decides to add, "This is not a court and there's no statute of limitations."

Fernando is lying on his bunk, staring into nothingness and three guards come rushing in. He looks surprised, is pushed up against the bars and held there while his cell is searched. They go straight to a place, inside his mattress, where he keeps his knife.

"This is all we wanted, Inez," The guard who is holding him, lets him go. "You're on you own now." All smile and exit as quickly as they entered.

Fernando is putting clothes into a large washer and seems to realize he is being watched. He turns in time to see a dozen inmates move in on him. He is taken down onto the floor and beaten with socks, which hold, each a bar of soap. When Fernando is barely conscious he is held face down, his shirt is torn away and while he is held, one inmate, with a fork prong, carves an unsophisticated, stick-figure tattoo of a bird on his shoulder. Fernando screams in agony, loud enough for guards to hear, but no help comes.

Fernando walks up to Dreamer. Fernando is badly beaten and bandaged, laying on an infirmary bunk. He looks angrily at Dreamer. Dreamer responds to the look. "You aren't dead. That's not because of your popularity or your skill. No one was sure that I wasn't going to protect you."

Fernando reaches toward his shoulder, where he was marked. "Is this all I get?"

Responding, as if hurt, "I told you I never forget my friends. Your time is almost up. When you get out, go and see a man named Armado. He will help you."

"How will he know you've sent me?"

Dreamer laughs mildly, "He already knows."

The day Fernando is being released a car drives up and stops near him on the sidewalk in front of Central Jail. He looks frightened at first and reaches into his pocket as if he has something concealed there. A man rolls down the window of the car and speaks. "Get in. Armado is ready to repay you."

Fernando gets into the vehicle, alone in the back seat and asks, "Where are we going?"

"To see Armado."

In a few blocks, this car pulls up to the bumper of another car and stops. Fernando gets out and walks up behind the other car. It is a white limo. The door of the limo opens and Fernando gets inside. An older man, Mexican and well dressed, is sitting inside, facing forward. He indicates to Fernando to sit opposite him on the rear-facing seat. Fernando looks frightened and resigned, much the same as he did on his first day in prison.

"Relax. If I wanted to hurt you, you wouldn't have gotten into the car. In fact, you would not have gotten out of the joint. You were a perfect target right where you were. Dreamer told me that he owed you one. I've come to pay the debt por mi amigo."

"How?" Fernando asks, relaxing somewhat at the irrefutable logic.

Armado reaches into his pocket, Fernando does likewise out of habit, fearing a gun, but the other pulls out a stack of papers. "He told me your name is no good anymore. So I'm here to give you a new one." Armado hands a few items to Fernando.

Fernando looks at a new passport, "Rudolfo Montillo. Who's this?"

"That's you. It's your new identity, if you want it." There is a long interval in the conversation to let Fernando consider his options. "I should tell you that if you don't accept this new identity, you'll probably be dead in a day or two."

"Do you know who?"

"Lloron had many friends. Dreamer was his friend once, just like you. One of those who still consider Lloron a friend might think he owes something to a dead man. It may be anyone. It may be nobody. You know that."

"What am I supposed to do? Should I abandon everything I know? Do you really have anything that you cannot leave behind? What about this tattoo? How will I take care of myself?"

Armado lets the new Montillo finish then continues. "You must leave everyone you know, everything before going to the joint, right now. If I were you, I'd get a tear tattoo under your left eye to let everyone know that you've done time. It will help keep people at a distance. We can take you to a new home. It's yours for a month; it's paid for in your new name. As for work, well, we can always find something for an amigo of Dreamer to do. You'll have work. As for the Paloma, you must do what people of our world have always done. You must make the best of it. Don't forget, Paloma also means *dove*. Perhaps you'll find religion!"

Looking down, Fernando shakes his head affirmatively accepting the new identity, then lifts his gaze to peer out of the tinted windows. He sees a chain-link fence, like the one that threw him into this memory. The image etches itself in his brain, like a metal spider's web that traces his life.

Montillo shivers slightly as the scene refocuses. He considers briefly going up to the youths and trying to dissuade them from using drugs. He rubs his shoulder then starts the car and drives away.

Chapter Eight
All Heroes Have One

Rico and Ron are pulling into another park. This one has a pool area, clearly visible from the lot where they park their car. The two men get out and scan the grassy area, near the pool. There are people laying on the grass near the pool, as there is very little deck. Most are young, under twenty. One of them calls out to the cops. He is called "SF" and another man sitting next to him, is called Joven. SF is not wearing a shirt.

"Hey, Panda? Aren't you going to say hello?"

"SF, I never knew you were so fat."

They all laugh as Rico and Ron walk over and Rico makes his first comments. "What are you boys up to...no good, as usual?"

"I don't believe this guy. You invite him over for a few friendly words. He insults you and then accuses you of doing something wrong. Why are cops so suspicious?" The young men laugh in a friendly way.

Joven takes up the banter, "If you want to hassle somebody, you aught to look over there." He points with his chin to the grassy area away from the pool. "Everyone there is doing something dirty."

Rico sits down on the grass, leans back and unbuttons his shirt to sun himself. "I don't feel like looking for bad guys right now." He whispers as he settles into a recline, hands behind his head.

Ron immediately gets uncomfortable, "I can't take this men taking off their shirts, sun-bathing stuff. I think I'll just take a look around." He starts to stroll casually away.

"So I hear you're after the one who did in one of our partners," SF says casually.

"That's right," Rico responds, with his eyes closed, still soaking up the sun. "What do you know?"

"Only that we shouldn't be talking to you."

"So, how come you're talking to me?"

SF looks at the others, scratches head and appears to have an idea," Because we're stupid?" He asks for clarification.

"Everyone is deaf, dumb and blind in this neighborhoods.: Rico laughs, then adds, "Ala brava, why aren't you guys afraid to be seen with me?"

Joven answers for the group, "Everyone knows that we don't know anything."

"And maybe because I was right. Maybe we're stupid and everyone knows that too," SF adds playfully.

Rico smiles broadly "For some reason, I believe you. And, you know what?" He shifts his body so that he is getting more direct sunlight, "I really don't care right now. This sun feels bitchen."

As Rico soaks up the rays, someone walks up and casts a shadow over his face. He opens his eyes as the person speaks. The man standing over him is a thirty year old Caucasian, dressed in overalls and a work shirt, looking like a farmer or a hippie."

"You guys want to buy some acid?" The hippie wants to know.

"No thanks," Rico responds quickly.

"How about some uppers or downers?"

"No, not today."

SF and the other man cover their faces, barely concealing muted giggles. The hippie walks away.

"Why don't you bust him, Panda?" Joven wants to know.

"Naw, he's just a dumb shit. I'm looking for guys who can tell me something of value. He's obviously not from around here. Anyway, I'm too comfortable right now and my partner has wandered off with the handcuffs."

"Go on," Joven coaxes.

"Yeah," SF chimes in. "If that were us, you'd have busted us ten minutes ago, before we even asked you to buy our dope. What…are you, prejudice against Mexicans?"

Rico sighs heavily and stands. He looks over at Ron and waves, but Ron doesn't see him. He takes a pencil from his pocket and writes a number on a piece of paper.

"Will one of you guys get Ron for me?" Rico hands the paper to SF. "…and call this number and tell them an officer needs back-up." SF takes the number and runs off. The other young man runs toward Ron. Rico moves toward the guy who has just tried to sell him drugs.

Rico moves reluctantly into position. The man is now sitting in the passenger seat of a station wagon. The car door is open and he has a coat over the front of his body. It is obvious that he has something in his hands, under the coat. Rico stops when he sees this, then quickly pulls out his gun, pointing at the man.

"Freeze motherfucker, or you're dead! I'm a cop! *Now*, put your hands were I can see them."

The man freezes , then slowly begins to obey orders. The coat drops from his body. As it does Rico takes aim, not knowing what's underneath. When the coat falls away, Rico sees that the hippie doesn't have a gun but is shooting a needle into his arm. Rico is stunned by disbelief.

Ron comes running up now and points his gun at the man from the opposite side of the car. Rico shakes himself from his dreamlike state and pushes the man to the asphalt.

"Come on man. This stuff is hot!"

Ron moves to search the car and SF and Joven run up as well. At this time other police autos also arrive.

SF is beside himself with excitement, "Wow! You caught him shooting up. Good one!"

Joven can also not believe what he's just witnessed, "That was so cool!"

Ron steps away from the car with something in his arms, "Well, look at this." He holds up a baby.

"What've you got here, Rose?" The arriving officer wants to know.

Rico is still looking over the situation in disbelief. "I don't know...But I'm really sorry I ever listened to these assholes."

Rico is speaking into a phone. He looks depressed. On the other end of the line is Sergeant Berman.

"Some asshole from Texas. Had his little girl in the back seat, I guess it was a parent kidnapping."

"Well, listen. I set up a meeting with Williams."

"What the hell for?"

"Because all we've got is this silly name, Paloma. Let's see if homicide has anything. Let's at least try and work with the guy."

"Fine. We'll meet you there." Rico hangs up and immediately rises to leave.

Rico and Ron walk into a sub-station where Berman greets them.

"Where is our favorite detective?"

"Right this way. He's waiting for us."

Berman leads the two cops to a small, nearby office. Detective Williams is sitting behind a desk, doing paper work, just as Rico remembered him from their first meeting. The three officers walk in and Williams looks up. "What the fuck do you assholes want?"

Berman takes the peacemaker lead, "We're supposed to be working on this Vito thing together. Have you guys been doing anything besides sitting on your butts?"

Williams responds calmly, "Alright, what do you have and what do you want to know?"

"What we know is that nothing but bunk on the streets, everybody and their sister has got some, but everyone's talking about the new stuff that's coming and hoping that it *isn't* bunk." Rico puts things in perspective.

Ron adds, "And, some jerk dealer they call Paloma is the *A Numero Uno* suspect in this case."

Williams smiles and snorts a scoff. "My, My. That's real fucking expert detective work. Did you guys find all this out by yourselves or did you have to pay your drug addled snitches?"

Berman steps back into the diplomat's role, "What's that supposed to mean?"

Williams continues, "I mean that we've been hearing the name Paloma for almost a year now. It's like a fucking joke on the streets. Every time something goes down and dirty, everyone starts yelling, 'Paloma did it.' It's gotten to the point that we don't know whether there really IS such a guy. You've got to wonder if anyone has enough time to do that many things wrong."

"You mean, you think that Paloma is just a make believe fall-guy?" Berman was truly curious.

"I didn't say that. I just mean you haven't given me anything new to work with. And, instead of trying to find out *if* Paloma is involved, you should be trying to find out *how* he's involved and who the hell he is. It's one of the best-kept secrets on the street. And, the street isn't a place where secrets are easily kept. Either this guy's a fucking master villain, or he's one of the luckiest assholes ever to drive a cop crazy." He looks directly at Rico. "This is perfect for you *Panda*. Every colorful super hero has one…"

"One what? An asshole?"

"No, both the good guys and the bad guys have one of those. Every superhero needs an arch-villain, a worthy adversary, *right*?"

"Do you have any other suggestions?" Ron asks, changing the subject. "Or are you just busting our chops because you don't know anything either?"

"Well, it seems obvious that there's big money getting ready to make a big buy. That's *yours* and Rose's expertise, isn't it? Who's got the bread that you'd like to see get buttered?"

While the other cops collectively scratch their heads, Rico comes up with a name, "Gonzales."

Williams turns instantly toward him, "Who's Gonzales?"

"Fredrico Gonzales," Berman proudly announces, glad to have information that Williams does not. "Big time bank roll for the family south of the border. Let's call him El Kabong!"

"We should probably keep an eye on him then," Williams instantly has become a team player.

"I'll take the first watch." Everyone looks at Ron, who has just spoken. "Maybe I can make him nervous."

Berman speaks to Rico, "I guess it's you and me, then."

"Just like always, *Kimosabi.*"

The little boy, Juanito Carlos finds Paloma is sitting in his usual spot, under the tree. Juanito sees him and after a moment, walks over. Paloma looks up. "What do you want? Has your *hepito* sent you?"

"No. I've come on my own. I want to try some chivas."

This even shocks Paloma, momentarily but he quickly composes himself, remembering his personal rule not to care and proceeds. "Chivas is expensive. Do you have the money to pay for it?"

"No, but I heard that you let some pay in other ways."

Paloma is amused, "What could a new born do for me?"

"I could deliver messages, carry things...I'd do whatever you want."

So far, the pusher is unimpressed, "Go back to your canton, before I tell your papa on you."

Juanito becomes angry and changes to warning tone, "I think you better give me what I want."

"Why do you continue to bark, little puppy?"

"If you don't let me have what I want, then I'll tell who you are. There are people who want to know who is the man here. I know some cops...The Panda would love to find out who's dealing here."

At first angry, then calming Paloma continues the conversation, "You little..." He stands, moves toward Juanito, and then stops himself. "O.K., I can see you got a little machismo. I admire that in a man. I was just testing you to see if you were strong enough to handle a fix." Paloma bends down, pulls up the grass and picks a special striped balloon, unlike the others, which are all solid in color. Paloma takes this one. Straightening back up, he hands it to Juanito. "This is for you."

"What do I owe you for this?"

"Haven't you heard? The first one is always free. It's a gift, from one friend to another. We can do business another time."

"Gracias!" The boy runs off.

Paloma calls out softly, with a sinister smirk, "Da nada."

In a small, hotel bungalow that rents by the week, Juanito rushes in through the door and finds that no one is home. He holds the balloon close to his body, like a precious secret. The room is quiet and empty, except for a single bed and few pieces of furniture. Juanito goes to a cupboard under the sink in the bathroom and pulls out a small, tied bundle. He places this on a kitchen table. He unwraps the bundle reveals a hypodermic kit. Methodically, he prepares an injection, following the steps as he's seen them hundreds of times before.

Now and then he holds completely still, obviously trying to be certain that he's not leaving anything out. He speaks the method to himself as he performs every function. First he takes all the pieces of the apparatus and spreads them out on the floor. There is a metal canister, some matches, a Sterno can, a needle and syringe, a rubber tube (for cutting off circulation), and a small piece of cotton.

Juanito puts the canister over the Sterno can, like a tiny barbeque, and lights the Sterno. He pours the contents of the balloon (after cutting it with a pair of scissors) into the canister. He adds water. After the contents of the canister begin to boil, he blows out the Sterno and prepares the syringe. He places the cotton (one small ball) into the mixture and then puts the needle into the cotton. He sucks the mixture through the cotton, using it like a filter. After he has filled the syringe he pushes the plunger just slightly to get out any air bubbles. Now, he ties the rubber tubing around his arm, tucking it under rather than knotting it, to make it easier to release. He stops here and looks at his forearm, with a little fear in his eyes, but proceeds.

He now must puncture his arm; he closes his eyes when he does this. He must now pull back on the plunger until some of his blood flows into the syringe. This tells him that there is a vacuum in the syringe. He pushes the plunger. At this moment he collapses, face down on the floor, hitting his face with a loud thud.

Rico and Berman are patrolling, "Sarge? Maybe our local snitches haven't gotten the full scoop. Maybe there's no communication between the downtown and the Valley, 'cause everyone is trying to stay low."

"I thought about that. But the guys in East L.A. and the guys here are all saying the same thing. A big sale is coming and it's the good stuff."

"But Vito had wandered all the way into L.A. Maybe we should be working down there."

Berman shakes his head. "No, we've got to stay in our own backyard. Our connections are here. If you think it's hard to get street people to talk when then know you, just imagine what it's like if you're a cop out of your jurisdiction."

Rico knows that Berman is correct, so he changes the subject, "You getting tired?"

"A little, but I'd like to keep riding a while. I keep expecting something to happen. Why? You got a date? You need to call Susie?"

"No."

Chapter Nine
The Difference between Fear and Honor

Rico comes out of a café where he'd gone to check for new information. Berman leans out of the car and hollers, "Hurry up, get in. There's a bust going down a few blocks from here"

Rico speeds up, gets into the car, and they move off as Berman explains, "Samuels was riding alone. He's got his claws into an out-of-towner. Let's go stick our noses in."

When they arrive at the scene, an older officer in his mid-forties has a suspect up against a wall. The suspect is Stranger, the pusher who led the undercover Morelli to his death with Paloma. Vic and Rico casually walk over and Berman recognizes the older officers, "How's it goin' Bud?"

"Just fine, Vic. What's up?"

"Just in the neighborhood. This is officer Rose. Why don't you let us take this one?"

Rico walks over and begins to search the suspect.

Bud, answering Vic, then comments to Rico, "Sure. I've already searched him. He's clean, except for some possible holes in his arms."

"If you don't mind," Rico says, as if speaking to no one. "I like to do my own searches."

"But, I said I already searched him. Don't you think I know how to do a simple search?"

Berman tries to cover up the breach of protocol, "Oh, don't mind him. He's just a little extra paranoid. He doesn't mean anything by it."

Bud relaxes as Rico goes through a standard search of Stranger. Slowly his hands slide up and down along the pusher's body. When he gets to Stranger's right leg, he stops at a small rip near the inside of the knee. Rico feels the leg carefully and then reaches into the hole of the fabric with the tips of two fingers. Slowly, he pulls out a knife.

Bud looks shocked and then angry. "What the?" Embarrassed, he rushes toward Stranger. "Why you mother…" and pushes Stranger to the ground, like a kid in a schoolyard dispute.

As Bud rears back and prepares to kick the suspect, Stranger instinctively covers up, waiting for the blow to land, and begins to plead his case, "I didn't know I had it. I forgot! I borrowed these pants, I swear!"

Rico grabs the shirt of the suspect and lifts him off the ground and out of the way of Bud, while speaking to the ruffled, veteran cop, "It's O.K.! We've got him now. You don't have to worry about this punk."

"Yeah, Yeah.," Berman tries to re-establish order. "We'll take him down and book him for you. *Marks Beef* and concealed weapon."

"Samuels is never going to forgive you for this," Vic tells Rico, when they are safely inside the car.

"I can live with a cop's hurt feelings, knowing that this asshole…" Rico points over his shoulder toward Stranger who is in back of car. "…won't be using one of us, or your BUD-dy as a pin cushion."

Berman nods, as this logic is irrefutable to a police officer.

At the station, Stranger is being placed into a small interrogation room. Rico and Vic stop, just outside the door for a moment, as Berman begins to strategize. "What do you think?"

"I'd like to squeeze him a little. One knife fighter usually knows another. One pusher usually knows another."

"He may even be the one we want. He's from the right area and there's the other two qualities you just mentioned."

"I don't think he's our guy, or I would have let Bud kick his ass. The knife is not the same type or quality that was used to take out Vito. Plus the way he had his blade hidden away, it didn't seem like he intended to use it much. Let's play it like we suspect him, apply some pressure and see what direction he squirms."

Both men take a deep breath and enter together. Stranger is seen sitting on a chair that is pushed up against a small table. Rico bulls his way into the room and toward the suspect. Berman stops him, standing in Rico's way as if protecting Stranger. "Cool off, Panda. We don't know that he's the one for sure."

"He's the one! We both know it, and I'm going to make him admit it and beg forgiveness, even if I have to kill him."

Stranger looks frightened, "Hey, what are you guys trying to pin on me?"

"I'll ask the fucking questions, asshole!" Berman pushes Rico back, further from Stranger then speaks directly to the suspect. "He's been under a lot of pressure lately. I don't think he'll hurt you as long as I'm here and as long as you're being straight with us." Rico relaxes and Berman moves in close and confidential. "We're just going to ask you a few questions. There's been a murder, and..."

Stranger interrupts. He doesn't need to hear anymore, "Hey, you guys are loco. I didn't murder anyone."

Rico rushes forward, putting his face next to Stranger's ear. "Who the hell said you did? Why are you defending yourself when you haven't been accused of anything...you goddamn liar? Got a guilty conscience?"

Stranger tries to rise, in anger, but Rico pushes him back hard. "You get up again and I'll squash you so hard, won't be *able* to get up."

"You'd better do what he says," Berman adds. "I think he means it."

Rico continues, "Now, I want your name and I want your street name. No mi des pedo. The name your mama gave you doesn't mean dog shit to me."

"I already told you. My name's Eduardo Lomas."

Rico doesn't allow any space for silence but immediately shouts, "What the hell is your *street* name?"

Stranger bows his head dejectedly, "I'm called Stranger."

"Stranger...This is Sergeant Berman. Everybody calls him *Sergeant Berman*. I'm called The Panda by my friends, but for now you can call me *Detective Rose*. I'm going to give you a little quiz. If you give me the right answers, everything's going to be cool. If not, I'm going to ask the sergeant to leave the room for a moment." Rico threatens in Spanish, "Cuando van a Sargento Berman, voy a enviarle al hospital."

"Si. Entiendo."

"So, let's start again. There was a cop killed in your neighborhood, last week. What do you know about it?"

"I know who *you* are. And, I know he was a friend of yours." Stranger continues when he is certain that Rico is satisfied. "He was new around there. We were all pretty sure he was a cop. He came on too strong."

"Who is *we*?" Berman wants to know.

"All of us, everyone who knows the streets."

"Dealers?" Rico clarifies.

"Some make a living that way."

"Are you a dealer?"

"No! I use some, and I've helped other locate a deal from time to time."

"Who is supplying these days??

"There are many who deal. I can't give you all of their names...*not for nothing.*"

Rico and Berman look at each other and realize they have to give a little. Berman takes up the interview. "What do you want?"

"I want to walk out of here. I want to help you and I want you to help me, that's all."

Rico acts as though a deal might be possible, "We can't let you walk. We'd need some awfully good stuff for a favor like that."

Stranger doesn't let what he sees as his narrow window of opportunity slip away, "I know who your friend was going to buy from on the night he was killed."

"You mean, you know who killed him?" Berman knew he was not yet in a courtroom, so he was allowed to lead the witness.

Stranger was not new to these games and weighs his words carefully, "I can tell you only who he was going to buy from on that night because I sent him to meet a dealer. I can't tell you what happened when they finally met, because I wasn't there."

"Don't waste anymore of our time!" Rico demanded. "Who was it? Give me a name!"

Stranger knows that this is the one piece of information that is keeping him out of a jail cell, but giving it up might cost him his life.

Berman presses forward, "Was it Paloma? Is that the name?"

Stranger looks concerned, but not shaken. "His name is Montillo."

"Montillo?" Rico rocks back on his heels. This name was completely unexpected.

"Does he have a street name?" Berman had learned the question from Rico and decided it was the right one for the moment.

Rico doesn't let Stranger respond, "Does the name Paloma mean anything to you?"

"I've seen a lot of pigeons, but the person I'm talking about is Rudolfo Montillo. I know where he lives."

"Where?" Rico and Berman speak at once.

"Is this valuable enough information?"

"Are you saying that this Montillo killed the cop?"

"I'm saying that Montillo was one of the *very* last person on Earth that your friend ever saw."

"How do you know that?"

"I saw them together with my own two eyes. I know this is the case."

"Did you see him kill Vito?"

"No. They met on the street and then walked out of my view *together*."

Berman and Rico move around the room, obviously thinking.

Berman speaks, "Well, I think this might get you off the marks beef. I can see what I can do about the other..."

"You know these aren't marks." Stranger displays his forearms once again.

"I don't know," Rico says. "Samuels isn't going to like it. If we only had something else, something to justify..."

"What do you want?"

Berman jumps back in, "We want you to do a buy from him, for us."

Later, Ron and Rico trade info and strategy via two-way radio while Ron sits outside a house that he has under surveillance, "Playing tag with this junkie was a lucky play. The guy just kept talking. We could hardly take notes fast enough." Rico is bringing Ron up to speed.

"Sounds too easy," Ron responds. "Anyway, that doesn't change what I just said. I'm not leaving until reinforcements arrive."

"Why the hell not?"

"Panda, I think we really struck it rich here. Something really big is goin' down."

"We already knew that."

"You don't understand. This is really big. I'm sure that these guys had something to do with what went down with Vito. This has something to do with why he was killed. You should see how freaked out they are. They're making themselves so fucking obvious, it's ridiculous! They *want* me to watch this house. They're *trying* to look suspicious, don't you see? They *want* me to stay here. That must mean that something's going to happen soon, and it's not going to happen here. So, as long as somebody stays here they'll think that we don't have any idea what's going on."

Rico shakes his head. "There must be something wrong with me. Maybe I'm tired too, but that sort of makes sense. O.K. We'll get somebody out there to replace you, but you gotta get some rest so you can work this warrant with me and Berman."

Ron sees something, "Would you look at that?"

"What's happening?"

"Another member of the party just showed. What a beautiful set of wheels." Berman seems to think of something. "Hey, Panda, you'd better get who you can to come over here right away. Call the Sarge. These guys are going to bolt and their not going in the same direction. I can't follow everybody."

"Alright, I'll see what I can do. You tell those guys to wait for us, O.K.?"

The phone is hung up. Rico redials, speaks into the receiver. "Sarge? Listen, Ron says we gotta drop over to Gonzales' house. Yeah, I know, but he's sure that something's goin' down and he wants reinforcements. Right." Rico looks at watch. "It's seven now, I'll meet you…" Rico realizes that he never went to check on Becky. "Oh, shit! Sarge, listen. I gotta make a stop. Can you get some guys together? Thanks. I'll meet you there." He hangs up.

Rico is just pulling up in front of a house. He gets out of his car and walks up the walkway. He knocks and a young Chicano answers; this is Poncho, Susie's brother.

Poncho acts surprised, "Hey, Rico? What's happening?"

Moving into the doorway, Rico replies, "Not much, bro. Where's your sister?"

"She's not here."

"Whatdaya mean? Is everyone alright?"

"Everyone's fine. She said to tell you that since she hadn't heard from you, she took care of things with…" Poncho strains to remember. "…a *Betty* or something."

"Becky?"

"Yeah, I think that was it. Anyway, she said not to worry and you can call her later, if you want." Poncho looks aside briefly, as if concealing information.

"Thanks bro." Rico turns to leave.

Poncho calls after, "Hey Rico?"

Rico stops and turns, "Yeah?"

"Never mind, just see you later."

Rico scrutinizes Poncho a moment; Poncho closes the door quickly, so as not to look suspicious.

Rico has just arrived and is getting out of car. Ron is still in the same place and there are two more cars parked out front. The sergeant is in one of them with another plain-clothes cop. The forth car has only one man in it. Rico walks over to Ron's car. "Did I miss anything?"

"The fun hasn't started yet."

"What's the plan?"

"I've seen five cars go in. That means that at least five can come out. We got four cops to chase at least five bad guys. So, as my math skills figure it, unless they are dumber than even I am, the bad guys can score one in a get-away."

"Great thinking partner. We *let* one get away in the chase and we're not even sure what they're up to in that house or which one we need to follow."

"Don't worry about a thing bro. We gotta let the bad guys think they're winning one every once in a while."

"Yeah? Why?"

"It's a long standing tradition."

In the living room of the Gonzales estate, a woman, elegantly dressed is looking out of the window. After a moment she closes the curtains and turns toward the group of men in the room. There are six men sitting and standing around. They include Gonzales and Paloma. Gonzales is a distinguished looking older Mexican, with finely trimmed gray hair, a mustache and wearing an expensive sharkskin grey suit. He sits in a large chair facing the other men. Paloma stands next to him.

Gonzales speaks to the woman, "How are our friends?"

"There's another one, now."

Paloma is pacing, uncomfortably, "How are we supposed to get out of here? This is too dangerous for all of us."

Another man, dressed in a suit asks, "Why did you have to bring us here, together? It must be obvious that something is going on. Even stupid cops can figure that out!"

"Don't worry about them! They're just fishing. They don't have anything on any of us, or they wouldn't be sitting outside if they did. They're just trying to make us nervous." Gonzales was the voice of reason.

"Well, it's working. I'm nervous." Paloma docsn't try to conceal his feelings. He makes his comment nonchalantly.

Gonzales speaks like a father to his son, "Don't be nervous. As long as everyone does what they've been told, we'll have no problems." His voice becomes stern. "This is a very important deal, to all of us. It has to be done the way I've described. If we can get this pipeline flowing, it will make us billionaires!"

Another man, dressed in white and wearing a panama hat seems to break under the pressure. "I don't like doing this. I don't like doing things differently than we used to. Why do we have to change? Aren't we all making more than enough money?"

Gonzales is angry, but decides to compose himself enough to establish order. "You don't have to like it! I say what you like. I pay for that privilege, and I say how this is going to go down. I've always told you what to do and when you did it you made money. Nothing has changed but the circumstances. Bigger shipments from new sources require special arrangements."

"But how," Paloma wants to know. "How are we going to get out of here?"

"There's only four of them." Gonzales states simply. "If we leave now, before anymore arrive, it will be easy. We all leave at once...that is YOU all leave at once. They can only follow four of you. Whoever doesn't get a tail, he comes back here."

"Comes back?" Paloma doesn't like the sound of this.

"Of course. I'll need a ride. I don't drive. It's too dangerous in this town. But, the deal is going to be made tonight. I can't do this by telephone; they've had that wired for years!" Gonzales laughs to himself, Then adds, "Is there anyone here who isn't in agreement? If so, tell me now. If you want out, we can cut you out." He looks at the man who questioned him earlier. "I must have a ride or the deal cannot be made. Agreed?"

All are silent, casting sideways glances. They know that to disagree would be to commit suicide. The point of no return had long since been passed.

Rico is now in his own car as are the rest of the men. Ron sees something and picks up the microphone to his radio. "This looks like it, boys."

Berman takes command, "Pick a car and ride it out; have fun."

Suddenly the gates to the estate open and cars begin to exit at a rapid pace. They head out in every direction possible and each car is followed by one of the cops. Paloma's car is one of the last to leave. Rico must decide which car he is going to follow and decides to let Paloma drive off, opting to catch the last car out of the gate.

Paloma looks into his rearview mirror and seeing that he is not being followed seems agitated. "Madre!" He drives for a few more seconds and then decides that he has no choice but to turn around.

When Paloma returns, he sees another car, belonging to one of the other dealers from the meeting, also pulling up. They look at each other confused, then the other car drives off. Instantly, Gonzales comes out, rushes to Paloma, who is scared. Gonzales gets in and the two men leave. The woman can be seen looking out the window.

Paloma drives fast, with an intent look on his face. The engine revs slightly and this concerns Gonzales, "Not too fast. We don't want to catch up to the others." Paloma slows the vehicle.

"It's lucky; you were the one who came back."

"Why's that?"

"I have special information for you. Someone is trying to set you up."

"Who? Why?"

"We both know why. I'm not sure WHO, yet. But, when I find out, you've always been a friend to me. Like a son. I'll take care of you." Paloma does not respond and after a long, silence, Gonzales points. "Turn here. Now there."

Paloma does as he is told.

Paloma is told to pull over and leave the engine running as Gonzales exits. He stands at the open passenger door of the car. "You don't need to wait. I'll get a ride back. It won't matter if the policia see me coming back. There's nothing anyone can do to stop this deal, now, thanks to you."

"It's you who deserves my thanks."

Gonzales looks embarrassed, closes the door and exits toward a nearby house. Paloma watches a moment then drives off.

In the midst of the chase, the sounds of cars speeding through the city streets, squealing tires and revving engines can be heard both on the two-ways radios and in the air.

Rico and Ron are still close to their respective suspects. The drivers of the cars that Rico and Ron are following are scared, even though they are completely clean.

Ron calls out over the radio, "These guys are crazy. What the hell am I supposed to do now, Panda? They've broken about every driving law there is."

"My guy must be related to yours." Engine and screeching tire sounds get loud momentarily. "Damn! He went up on two, goddamned wheels! Two wheels! He's a freaking stunt driver."

"Where the hell is Berman? I can't raise him on the mic and I thought I saw the car he was following, doubling back toward the Gonzales house."

"Fucking Berman! He's probably on his way home right now. He probably lost his man and decided to pack it in."

"Rico, I'm giving up too. I'm too damn tired for this shit and these guys are just decoys."

"O.K. Sullivan. I'm not into the paperwork on a reckless driving bust either…Sarge? Hell! Where is Berman?"

Berman is still following his chosen car, but this chase is a direct counterpoint to the ones that Ron and Rico are involved with. The car that Berman is following is driving extremely slowly. The lead car turns a corner, running a stop sign at about two miles an hour and proceeds at this pace. A motorcycle pulls up to Berman's window. It is a cop's, on duty bike.

Berman rolls down his window, flashes his badge out and continues to drive. The bike cop raises his voice slightly to converse with Berman, "What are we doing?"

"We're following that car."

"The slow one? Why?"

"Because he left the house."

"What house?"

"The house we were watching."

"Are their other team members? Where are they?"

"I don't know. My radio isn't working."

"Are they doing something *really* illegal? What're you trying to get them for?"

"It's not important. Maybe you could stop them for driving too slow?"

"Can we do that? Do you really want me to?"

Berman looks at the other cop in disbelief. "Shit!" He steps on the gas and squeals a wide U-turn in front of the motorcycle cop.

On a beautiful farm there are workers, in the distance, cultivating a crop which is not clearly visible. Suddenly, a figure, dressed in gray, khaki, walks out of a shack with one of the workers. We see that he holds a sub-machine rifle. He is dressed in semi-military clothes and is not one of the farmers. He is watching over the farming operations.

Several other men, dressed and armed similarly, surround the entire pasture, at various posts. The workers don't seem to care about the armed men and the men with the rifles don't seem to be concerned with the farmers. A farm house is in the distance, but is partially constructed of canvas. One of the canvas walls is a flap that has been lifted. Inside we see chemistry apparatus and two, Caucasian males. Everyone else is obviously a Mexican farmer. They are dressed in the cotton muslin, typical for peasants. There is a large empty space between the barn and the cultivated fields. This empty space connects to a dirt driveway that leads to a dirt road that surrounds the fields. The armed men stand along the roadway, in the distance. In the middle-foreground is a group of farmers, who are over-seeing the operations of both the chemists and the field workers. They all have extreme looks of satisfaction on their faces. One of these men is Hernando Escanza. He is relatively the central figure here. He is also, slightly more well dressed than the others, with a suit jacket over his work shirt. The conversation is in Spanish.

"It is a beautiful crop [Es una cosecha Hermosa]," one of the farmers says.

"Yes. Truly it is a fine crop, our best yet," comments Escanza.

"And more profitable than when we used to grow corn," says another farmer to Escanza. "When will Miguel be here to give us the money?"

"He'll be here. He said it was all set. He'll be here."

The men begin walking toward the barn. The two young, college or high school students, who are the chemists, are working with the apparatus. They stop and greet the farmers as they enter.

Chemist One greets the trio, "Hello, Signor Escanza. It's an honor to see you out here."

"I still love to come to the fields and smell the soil and the clean air." He leans close to the others. "I even love the smell of manure," he whispers.

"And the fragrant flowers?" The second chemist asks.

"Yes, the poppies are much sweeter smelling than people give them credit for. Is it ready?"

"It's in the vault. " Chemist One points with a nod.

Escanza smiles and nods and the committee of farmers walk toward the vault. It is not very burglar proof. Escanza kneels, turns the dial a few times and opens the vault. He slowly, nonchalantly removes two large plastic bags of white powder, and, here exhibits them lovingly to the group.

Through the opened canvas flap, a car is seen to drive into the open area near the barn. The farmers look and begin to move.

A man is just getting out of the car. He looks pretty much like the others. Escanza calls out, "Miguel! How nice to see you."

"Hernando, you old goat. You stay away from the village too."

"I've been very busy, lately but I'm here now!"

"I understand," Miguel turns his attention to the fields. "It's a very beautiful crop."

Escanza is beaming with pride, "Thank you. Here is the fruit of the harvest you've come for." He hands the packages he just retrieved to Miguel.

Miguel takes the packages and examines them only briefly. "They are beautiful." Miguel walks back to his car, takes out a briefcase and hands this to Escanza, who remembers his manners, "Would you like to join us for some food? Some cerveza perhaps?"

"I was hoping you'd ask." He puts the packages into the trunk of the car. "I'm a little hungry *and* thirsty. How's your wife?"

"As sweet and as mean as always, just like every man's wife." All laugh, including the young chemists.

Miguel is just getting into his car and driving away from Escanza and the others.

The second farmer says, "I like Miguel. I wish he could have stayed longer."

"Yes," Escanza agrees, "But he had to make his appointment."

Late that night, Miguel's car stops at a lonely looking mailbox. There is nothing else around as far as Miguel can see. He turns off the engine, gets out, looks in both directions on the road, walks to the box and drops the packages into it. He returns to the car and drives along the road and out of sight.

Twelve hours later another car drives into view. This one has two men in it, both Mexicans in casual, modern but generic looking uniforms. One man gets out and goes to the box. He has a key though he is clearly not the postman. He opens the box and removes the packages, returns to his car and drives off in the same direction that Miguel did.

That same night, in a border town motel, a numbered door opens to a hand knocking. The men from the car are inside. They greet the person at the door.

As the sun begins to rise, the two men are driving slowly through the streets. They pass a Mexican, federal-police car. There is no exchange of words or expression between the two cars, but as soon as it is clear that the *federales* have seen the two men, the driver accelerates quickly and races for the border. There is a brief chase scene here as the two cars head directly for the border and across it. U.S. officials watch in disbelief, shaking and scratching their heads. They watch as the two cars head into U.S. territory, past them and over the horizon.

In the interior of the two cars are shown, neither pair of riders seems overly concerned. Across the border now, the chase has proceeded to a desolate road where both cars decide to stop the chase. The Mexican police car turns off its siren, all of a sudden and the lead car—with the two men--pulls to the side of the road. The *federales* walk casually to the waiting car and the other car's occupants get out and wait for the police to come up. When they get to the car, they do not concern themselves with the two men, but look around. Then, one of them returns to the police car. He comes back a few seconds later with the packages of heroin that we saw the other two men with previously. While the others watch, this officer opens a compartment, in the frame of the car, beneath the door of the driver's side. He pushes the packages inside and closes the space. At this time, sirens are heard in the distance, getting closer.

The two Mexican police, reacting to the sound, take charge of the two men, as if they are arresting them. Two American, border officers arrive in separate cars. The man who is being arrested curses at one of the Mexican officers, in Spanish. He is pushed, rather harshly by the *federale's* foot, into the Mexican police car. The Americans walk up, casually viewing this scene. They converse in a combination of English and Spanish.

"Is everything alright here?" The American border patrolman wants to know. [Todo esta bien aqui?]

The first federale responds, "Si. Muy bueno."

The second federale speaks, after putting the two men into the back of the federal car. "They had false papers with them. [Tenian papeles falso] We'll take them back with us and deal with them. [Nosotros os llevarmos para tras a reglarnos con ello]"

The second American officer enquires, "What about their car?"

"I have already notified your impound service. They are coming to pick it up now. It's a gift." The first federale smiles slyly.

"Fine, we'll escort you back to your country." All begin to move toward their respective autos.

The first federale responds to last comment, while still moving into his car. "If you wish. [Si cares.]" They leave the U.S. with the drug-vehicle parked alongside the road.

Later, in the afternoon, a tow truck pulls into the picture and parks in front of the car. A young man gets out and walks to the driver's side of the vehicle. He opens the door, looks to the horizons then removes the packages from their hiding places. He takes them to his truck, on the passenger side.

Inside his truck the young man lifts a battery from the floor and places it on the seat. He pops the top of the battery revealing a hollow space inside the fake batter and he puts the packages inside. He replaces the false top, gets a second battery from the floor, repeats the process then returns to the driver's side of his truck. He begins to hook up the abandoned car for towing.

After dropping the car off at the federal impound yard, the driver takes a few short turns, onto a main street. Looking through the windows of the car, he sees a road sign that reads LOS ANGELES, with an arrow in one direction and SAN DIEGO, in the other. He turns toward L.A. and smiles, looking down at the batteries that are still on his floor.

Stranger is on the telephone. The sound is that of muffled ringing at the other end. The receiver at the other end clicks and Stranger begins to speak immediately. "Paloma, I tried to find you at your usual place, but you weren't there. What's wrong?"

Paloma speaks from the other end of the line, "What do you need *me* for?"

"I'm looking for a fix."

"Your friends will have to wait, or deal with someone else for a few days."

"This is not for one of my friends," he says sadly. "It's for me."

"Stranger, you're not strung out are you?"

"Yes. I started a few weeks ago, chipping a little from the spoons I sold." Desperately he adds, "Mi carnal, I think I need a fix badly."

Paloma is confused, torn emotionally, but this doesn't come across the receiver to Stranger, "Why me? Go to some other dealer!"

"You know I can't do that. If I have to buy from someone else, like this, they'll know I need it. You know what that means…You're the only one I can trust. You are mi hermano, mi padre. You've taught me everything I know. I've done everything for you. You've got to help me. I just need a little, until I can kick it."

Paloma deliberates then decides, "You can't come here. Meet me at my spot. I'll be there in an hour."

Smiling, then acting as if in great need, "I'll be there. Gracias, mi carnal."

Stranger walks down the street, on the sidewalk. As he passes a gray van, parked on the opposite side of the street, he gives a quick glance over his shoulder.

Inside the van there are two undercover cops and a great deal of electronic equipment. There is a tape recorder and a small camera. The camera is pointed through a small, one-way window at the rear of the van. Stranger has positioned himself in front of the camera.

Standing nearby we see Paloma. He and Stranger stand and look at each other only briefly and then Stranger moves toward Paloma. Paloma is near his usual tree.

"Do you have it?" Stranger asks eagerly.

"Aren't you even going to thank me, as your amigo for coming here?" Paloma acts hurt and annoyed.

"I'm sorry. I'm hurting though. I can hardly think straight."

"Let me see your arms." He takes Stranger's arms and begins to examine them, revealing recent marks. Paloma's face shows a mixture of sadness and disbelief.

"I have what you need around the corner."

"Why aren't you dealing from your spot?"

"I don't want anyone to see me or you." Paloma begins walking and Stranger follows. "I told my customers that I was not dealing right now. If they see me with you, it will look bad for both of us."

Inside the van two plain clothes cops discuss the situation, "Where the hell are they going?"

"They're moving around the corner, into the alley. They're out of camera view, what do we do?"

The first cop holds an earphone to his ear. "We still have audio...It'll be enough, especially if we can score him with the laundry money."

In the same alley that Vito was killed, Paloma stops abruptly and turns toward Stranger. Stranger looks around and wonders what's going on.

"Where do you have it?"

"I had to keep it in a special place." Here he puts his finger down his throat and gags himself. He pulls a long string from the inside of his mouth. One end of the string is tied to a tooth, the other end, obviously, was in Paloma's stomach. Stranger looks a little sick to his stomach then gets control of himself. Paloma reveals that a single balloon is tied to the end of the string that was in his stomach. He hands the balloon to Stranger, who takes it, but reluctantly.

Reacting to Stranger's show of emotion, Paloma comments, "If you truly need it, it won't matter where it's been."

Stranger tries not to show concern, "Is it the new stuff or is it bunk?" There is no answer. "Is the new stuff in yet?"

"Don't worry, I'll let you know when it arrives. This is all I have for you, now."

Stranger presses, prying, "When do you think the new stuff will be here?"

"Are you that bad off that you're already worried about your next fix before you've even shot this? It'll be here soon. Get going now. I have to jam."

Stranger turns and starts to walk away. Paloma watches him a moment then calls after him. "Haven't you forgotten something?"

Stranger stops and seems to realize he's forgotten to pay. "I'm sorry…" Not wanting to use the name Paloma he responds, "..Montillo."

Paloma looks as if he's been struck. Stranger has never called him Montillo before. He knows at this moment for certain that Stranger is the snitch. Until this moment, he was not sure.

Stranger sheepishly hands him the money.

"Never mind," Paloma doesn't take the money. "It's a gift. This one's on me."

Stranger panics. "I insist. You've gone out of your way for me." He pushes some marked money into Paloma's hand. "Please, do me this favor and take the money. It will make me feel a little better."

Paloma does not argue further. He stares at Stranger sadly as Stranger exits. As soon as he is gone, Paloma walks to the nearest dumpster, crumbles the money and buries it in the trash.

Paloma is just finishing dialing the phone in one of many phone booths he uses as his offices. After a moment, he speaks into the receiver. "May I speak to Mr. Gonzales?"

"Who is calling, please?" The female lookout asks at the other end.

"Tell him it's his driver from last night."

Paloma hears the woman getting muffled instructions at the other end, which she relays, "You are to go to the Star Invaders Arcade in half an hour."

The phone is hung up without another word.

Paloma enters and sees Gonzales playing a game. He approaches him. Gonzales acts excited about the game. He then speaks to Paloma as he continues to play. "Be brief. I have a friendly police officer meeting me to take care of the unfriendly Panda for us."

"You mean you have hired a cop as an assassin? Bravo! I too need an enemy disposed of…The Stranger."

"It will be done."

At this point a plainclothes, Hispanic officer, enters with some sort of badge slightly exposed under his coat. He and Paloma look at each other briefly but intently. The cop recognizes Paloma, but can't place him.

Rico is seen putting items onto shelves in a small grocery store that his family owns. His father, in mid-fifties, looks on proudly.

"It's so good having you here to help me."

"I'm all yours today pop."

"I wish it could always be like this. Someday when you get this cops and robbers stuff out of your system."

"Come on dad. Let's not get into this shit again, O.K.? Although it's hard to argue with you when I'm on my knees and wearing an apron."

Rico's father shakes his head affirmatively and giggles to himself. Just then another employee comes up and speaks to Rico. "Hey, Ricardo. There's a call for you."

"Thanks," Rico rises and walks past his dad to a very small, back room office. There's a phone on a table, which is used as a desk. There are piles of papers on the table, a cheap lamp and a phone. The receiver is off the hook. Rico enters and picks it up then switches to a speaker as he sits in the folding chair behind the table.

"Yeah?"

"Panda," Ron's voice is heard. "Berman just called. He wants us to go down and check out some dead meat that they just shipped in to the freezer."

"The morgue? Now? Who bought it?"

"Berman thinks it's your snitch. He's trying to run down the warrant, so you gotta go and identify the body."

Rico looks down hall, through door, as if thinking. "I hate this shit." Then, after a pause, "O.K. I'll meet you."

Rico's father walks in as Rico hangs up the phone.

"I gotta leave for a little while. I'm sorry."

"You said you were off work today."

"I'll just be a little while, I swear. I'll be back." Rico reaches into a cardboard box, retrieves his gun and badge and takes off his apron as he exits.

Chapter Ten
The Players Without a Scorecard

The morgue is brightly lit but stark, white and sterile looking. There are several double doors on each side of a wide, long hallway. At the center of the hallway, near the foreground of the scene, are a single couch and a single chair. It is a feeble attempt at creating a waiting room affect in an empty hallway.

When Rico arrives, Ron is sitting on the couch, which is against the wall. Ron spots Rico and stands, waiting for his partner to get within proper earshot. He doesn't want to speak loudly with all the dead bodies nearby. "Doc Crovatin's on duty. He wants you to go right in."

"Don't give me that bullshit! You're going coffin diving with me."

"Right." Ron gestures for Rico to lead the way.

As the two cops come through the doorway they see a relatively large room with cabinets on two of the walls. These cabinets are numbered and obviously contain dead bodies. At the far end of the room is a man, tall, overweight and gray, wearing a red flannel long-sleeved shirt under a short sleeved, unbuttoned white smock.

This is Doc Crovatin, who is on the telephone. Between the doctor and the two cops (off to one side) is an examination table (like an operating table). There is a sufficient amount of medical looking equipment to establish that this is the place where the bodies come to be filed away, before they are identified.

The two cops stand in the room and rustle nervously, waiting for the Doctor to finish his conversation. "Alright then, bring him down." The Doc hangs up, looks at Rico and Ron and smiles.

"How's it going Doc?"

"Same old thing. It's kinda nice to see two people standing upright, for a change."

Everyone cringes at the feeble joke. Crovatin becomes embarrassed, then serious, "I understand you may know one of our customers."

Rico looks toward the cabinets. "I'm willing to take a peek."

"What about your partner?"

"Yeah, he wants to look too. Like you said, we're partners."

The doctor walks to the cabinets, chooses one and pulls it out like a long drawer. There's a body inside, with a tag on the foot. The face is covered with a sheet. The doctor pulls away the sheet.

"That's the bastard." Rico turns immediately away after recognizing Stranger.

"Who was he?" Crovatin asks pointedly, while closing the drawer.

"I knew him as Stranger. I'm sure we've got the stats on him in our files."

As Rico is making his last comment, in background an examination table, like the one in the room, is being wheeled in. A man, about twenty-five is pushing the cart. The man's name is Maxwell.

Absentmindedly, Maxwell suddenly notices the others, "Oh, I didn't expect to see anyone standing upright." Everyone cringes.

"Maxwell, this is officer Rose and officer Sullivan," Crovatin makes the introductions and Maxwell nods, pushing the gurney past the group.

"What're you guys doing up so early? Don't you just come out at night?"

"They had to identify some dealer's body."

Maxwell reacts violently, "A dealer got his? Good!"

"Why'd you say that?" Ron wants to know.

Maxwell pulls back the sheet that's covering the body he's just wheeled into the room, "I've got a special grudge against dealers tonight."

By the time Maxell finishes his sentence, Rico sees that it is the body is that of Juanito Carlos. "Every time I see one of these overdose victims, especially one this young, I feel like getting a gun and going after those bastards myself."

Rico's eyes are white as he recognizes Juanito.

Crovatin notices Rico's condition. "You'd better grab your *partner*. I think he's going to faint, and I've never had a good bedside manner with the living," he says to Ron.

Rico yells to no one in particular, "Goddamn bastards!"

Ron grabs and shakes his friend. "What's the matter with you? (realizes) Do you know him?"

"I busted him a long time ago. He's the reason I met Susie."

Maxwell says matter-a-factly, to Crovatin, "His name's Juan Carlos. He's been dead for about three days." Everyone pays close attention now. "His father's a hype, too apparently. He was out on a binge for a while and didn't come home to find his kid until tonight."

Rico seems to let this statement sink in and then, boiling to a rage rushes out of the room.

"You don't need us anymore?" Ron asks the doctor as he follows Rico out the door.

In the hallway Rico is looking both angry and embarrassed. "How you feeling?" Ron waits for a shrug of understanding from Rico. "Maybe this isn't a good time to tell you, but Berman called after I talked to you."

Rico is suddenly interested, "Yeah?"

"He got the warrant on this Montillo character. Seems to be a lot of agencies and just plain volunteers interested in helping out on this one. He wants us to meet him at the station in an hour. We're forming a special unit."

"It's going down NOW?"

"No time like the present. Are you in?"

"Of course I'm in, asshole." Rico looks toward the doors of the examination room. I've never been so *in*, in all my life. I just gotta call my dad, first. He'll kill me if I don't. I promised to let him know before I do *any* warrants. You know."

"Pop, I'm sorry, but…" Rico was saying to his father over the telephone. The emotion in his father's face is of supreme importance here. His father is feigning anger, but seems to be more sad and worried than his words let on. "But, you said you'd be back. What could be so important? I really need you here. Couldn't you just miss this one time? For me? Alright Ricardo. Try and be careful. Oh, sure, sure, it's not dangerous...you be careful. You come by and eat tonight. It's O.K. It's O.K., I'll have your mother keep something warm for you. You just come by whenever you're through." Rico's father hangs up the telephone.

Rico exits an official looking building and enters the car, where Ron is waiting for him.

"I spend a lot of time in parking lots waiting for you, I realized," Ron says to his partner as Rico slams the door. "All taken care of?"

"I talked to my dad," Rico pauses to reflect then seems to come into the moment, "Well, let's go!"

"We're off!"

While driving Rico lifts his shirt and begins to undo a bullet proof vest that's underneath. Ron looks over at Rico with disapproval, so

Rico comments on his actions. "It is so damn hot today. I can't stand it." He tosses the vest into back seat.

"My, my Panda. You look positively naked without your armor. Isn't this a violation of one of *your own rules*? I don't think I ever saw you without your vest and you always told me that violating your own safety rules is the first step toward disaster. You're not getting sloppy in your old age, are you?"

"Just drive, will you? How dangerous could this be with all the coppers we'll have working this thing? I've got a sea of blue to shield me."

Ron smiles and shrugs.

Paloma is standing next to his car. It is parked on the side of the road, in a suburb, and the hood is up. He is looking restlessly up and down the street. At one point a police car (black-and-white) pulls up and the officer rolls down the window and calls out.

"Do you need any help?"

"No, thanks. I just called a tow truck, Officer. He'll be here any time."

"Alright, we'll come back by here in about half an hour to check on you. I've had to wait for days for tow trucks to show in this part of town."

Paloma smiles and waves as the black-and-white drives off. He begins to scan the horizon again and suddenly sees something in the distance. The same tow truck that made the pick up at the border is coming into view. It pulls up, along side of Paloma's car and hooks up battery cables, before saying a word to Paloma. Paloma looks upset.

"What took you so long?"

The driver is unimpressed. "Listen, asshole, this isn't triple A. Do you want your shit or don't you?"

Paloma stands and stares and the driver goes to the passenger side of his truck and gets out a share of the heroin that has now been put into small balloons and into small packages. Before giving them to Paloma he stops.

"Where's the money?"

Paloma reaches into his shirt and takes out an envelope, handing it to driver. The driver hands over a package. "Aren't you going to count it?"

"Why should I? If it's not all here, you'd be crazy. Gonzales would put you and everyone in your familia *out of business* forever."

"But, how do you know I'm the right guy?"

The driver unhooks the cables and gets into the truck. "You think that the big man would hand over this much shit to an amateur? I know what everyone of my connections looks like. I know who you are, where you've done time and the names of everyone who'd like to see you dead." The driver shakes his head in disbelief. "Here's a little bit of advice for you. Take the time to learn who you're dealing for."

Paloma watches the truck drive off, then pulls down the hood, gets into his own car, placing the package under his seat and drives away, too.

In a very small conference room, Williams joins eight other plain clothes officers. A Chicano cop named Contrares, pacing nervously, speaks. "When are we going to get this bust moving? Let's put it down now! I wanna bust some ass."

The other officers in room look at Contrares with disgust especially Williams. Ron and Rico now enter the room with Berman.

"Hey look at the kid," Contrares comments when Rico comes into view, ignoring the fact that his own partner is much younger and right out of boot camp.

"Hey Rico, how's it going?" Another officer ignores Contrares and bumps fists with Rose.

"O.K. Smitty. How you doing?"

Rico leans to Berman and whispers, "Who the hell is that asshole?" He points to Contrares.

"That's Contrares. He's an old Vet from East L.A. division. Don't worry about him. He's just trying to overcompensate for his partner."

"All right girls," William interrupts the private conversations. "Let's get the party started by making sure everyone knows each other." He turns to Rico. "Detective Rose, I think you know everyone except Contrares and Vasquez." Williams casually points to each in turn. The three officers acknowledge each other as Williams continues, "We've already picked teams. The Panda's with me." Rico looks surprised. "…And you two Valley characters," He points to Ron and Berman. "…Can ride together. Berman, you know how this is going down?"

"Yeah, I got all the paper on it."

"O.K. then let's go do it."

All begin to exit. Ron turns to Rico and winks. "Have fun with your new partner." Ron laughs as Rico cringes.

In the police parking lot it is an explosion of vehicles, as cars start, misfire and drive off. Rico is standing next to his and Williams' assigned vehicle. Williams gets in the drivers seat opening the door for Rico. There is noticeable tension between them, as Williams attempts to break the ice, "I'm glad I got hooked up with you Rico. At least you know your butt from your burrito. Some of those fuck-heads in there are perfect idiots. Did you hear Contrares? What an Adam Henry! And, who let the Boot, Vasquez in on this?"

"If you don't like those two, why did you pick 'em for the team?" Rico thought to himself, but instead of letting these words out of his mouth, he said instead, "You didn't like him either?"

"Like him? I just about puked every time I heard him say that he wanted to *get goin' and bust some ass*. He couldn't bust anyone's ass but his own, the little pansy." Williams starts the car. "This tin can sounds like shit. Have we got everything we need?"

"Seems like it."

Williams starts to back car out then stops suddenly. "Hey do you know where we're suppose to be going?"

"No, I threw away the *D* sheets as soon as they were handed to me."

"I knew you were my kind of cop." Williams guns the engine and gets ready to move when a man on a bicycle rides up toward the driver side of the car.

"Officers! Oh, officers!" Williams becomes enraged at the bicyclist for no apparent reason. He jams the car in reverse and burns rubber, directly back toward him, slamming on the brakes and stopping within inches of the bike. "What the fuck do you want?" He calls out the open window.

The bicyclist is quite frightened, "You *are* police officers aren't you?"

"Do we fucking look like cops? Does this piece of shit look like a cop car? What the hell's the matter with you?" Williams now maneuvers the car toward the street, fish tailing as he burns rubber. Rico and Williams turn to each other and burst out laughing.

"I think you might be crazier than I am!" Rico observes then adds, "Hey I better get on the radio and find out where we're supposed to be going." He attempts to use the radio but realizes it is not working. "I don't think the radio is working," Rico states matter-a-factly, almost unconcerned.

"You dumb shit, you don't know how to use the fucking thing." Williams takes the mic out of Rico's hands. He fiddles with it and the controls of radio then throws the mic down. "It doesn't work. Great fucking God and all His angels. We're professionals, we should expect equipment that is operational!"

"We should know where the fuck we're going!" Both Rico and Williams laugh, then Rico adds. "We could go back and get directions, looking like complete jerk-offs or we could just head towards the general area. I think I remember where that is."

"Fine fucking thinking! What the hell did you think I was going to do? Just drive around until I saw something I liked?" Williams races past the freeway on-ramp. "God damn I missed the ramp!"

"Be careful. There's a CHP sitting on his bike at that ramp."

"So what? What's he going to do arrest two crack cops like us for driving like assholes in the line of duty? Even that fuck-head on the bike could tell we were cops in this fine police cruiser!"

Williams spins the car in a short arc, cuts off several other cars heading in opposite direction. Rico picks up the mic of the dead radio as they drive past the CHP Officer, hoping to indicate that they are police. The CHP watches in disbelief as Williams races by him, onto the freeway.

"I can't believe it. You've always been such a jerk to me. Everyone says you're an asshole, but you're not so bad. You just don't have any people skills."

"Hey, Rico, don't go spreading that kind of talk around. I don't want people to think I'm *nice*. I want them to hate me, to leave me alone. That's the only way I'm going to get anything done on the streets."

Rico nods in agreement, "Hey, I think I see one of our guys just ahead!"

"Don't worry, I'll just hop into the diamond lane and drive like hell to keep up with this guy, hoping that he is one of ours." Williams steps on the gas even harder, locking his arms at the elbows to indicate that he is concentrating on his driving now. "Oh, hell, just when I was about to catch 'em." Williams looks into the rearview mirror and tilts his head backward in a silent gesture. Rico looks back.

"You'd better stop."

The CHP is pulling them over. Williams exhales his disgust and pulls to the side of the road. Immediately, Rico jumps out, and rushes to CHP bike with his badge hanging out of his wallet. "Hey, were *real* cops, serving a warrant, protecting a serving."

The CHP officer doesn't even get off his bike. "Go on, get the hell out of here."

Rico turns and returns to car at a run, jumping in, hoping to catch up with the vehicle they were following.

"Were off again and we're going to cut 'em off at the pass!"

"What pass?"

"I just remembered what was written on the detail sheet." Williams replies and moments later, they catch up to other car pull them over.

Williams pulls up along side of other cop car and yells through the window. "We don't have a radio!"

"Use your C.C.," the other cop responds.

"We don't have a C.C. Let us use yours," Rico answers.

The other officer shuffles in their glove box a moment and hands a small walkie-talkie through the window to Rico.

"Thanks."

Williams hardly waits for Rico's hand to fully grasp the walkie-talkie then races off, growling, "It's great to be a professional law enforcement official and be given equipment that works. Hey!" Williams slams on the brakes and yells back to the other cops. "Hold on a minute. Where are you guys heading anyway?"

The other cop seems a little confused but yells back. "The Baldwin Park pad. Aren't you two supposed to be near the freeway as back up?"

"Yeah, Yeah, sure. We're going there now." Rico announces, then thinking he adds, "Hey, is there anything specifically we should know? Any new developments?"

"I guess Contrares picked up the suspect already. He's in a brown, sixty-nine Plymouth. He's just driving around L.A. He doesn't seem to be going anywhere."

"Just like every low rider," Williams mutters.

Just then, Rico realizes that his ignorance has been properly displayed, but that the other cops are not busting him. "O.K. well, thanks and let's get moving!" He rolls up the window and Williams drives off at a more moderate pace. "Good work, Panda. At least now we know where the hell we're going. Rico pulls out a map from the glove box, examines it.

"Hey, I think I just remembered we're supposed to be at this onramp, going north." Rico points to place on map.

Chapter Eleven
The Little Matters of Life and Death

In a few minutes Rico and Williams' car is pulling into an open field on the side of a freeway. The field is part of a large farming complex of fields. There is a bunch of bushes, lining the road, between the street and the field. Williams backs into a clump of these bushes partially concealing the car and stops.

"This is it?" Rico asks.

"Sure this is it," Williams says with confidence, ignoring that Rico was with him just minutes before when they had no idea where they were going. "What's wrong with this?"

Rico shrugs and Williams adds in a tone of a wise old master, tutoring a student, "Better make yourself comfortable. This could take a while."

Both men settle in for only a few second, then Rico asks, "Know any funny stories?"

"Of course I know some funny stories; what the hell do you think I am? Some sort of idiot? Everyone knows some funny stories."

"Well?"

"Well, what?"

"Can you tell me one of them?"

The two cops are now laughing hysterically, as if a joke has just been told. While their laughter is just beginning to subside, Williams starts to become aware that a number of people are now walking past the car (from back to front) as if appearing out of the fields. There are young and old, men and women. Williams becomes suddenly serious, is about to react but then Rico becomes aware of these people and calms his partner, "Don't worry you dumb shit. These are just the illegals from the lettuce fields. "

"Oh, my God!" Williams responds as if truly terrified. "Look at all the goddamn Mexicans! Rico, you've got to do something. Talk to them in something other than English. They're your people."

Rico calls out the window in Yiddish, "Sholem aleykhem mine khavern zikh. Zayt azoy gut nite shatn undz!" And then he starts to crack up. Just then, while Williams continues to shrink into his seat and cower as if he's frightened, a call comes over the CC. It is the voice of Contrares. *"We lost him."*

Williams and Rico stare at one another and stop laughing at the same time. Williams picks up the C.C. "You what?"

"We lost the suspect."

Then, the voice of Berman comes over the air, "What the hell is going on?"

"We're near the corner of Ninth and Western," Contrares continues. "He made a right turn in front of us and then he was gone."

Rico turns to Williams and shakes his head in disgust. "I knew that guy was an asshole. Goddamn it!"

"Panda, is that you? You should tell your new partner to take his thumb off the send switch. Are you nearby?"

Rico grabs the CC from Williams. "We're on our way. Contrares? Meet you in five. Stay where you are."

Williams is starting the car even before Rico is finished speaking. "Goddamn assholes don't know how to follow a goddamn suspect." Then Williams adds, turning to Rico, as if editorializing. "Rico, I hate working with assholes. We lost 'em. They made one of those fancy driving maneuvers. What do you call 'em? A RIGHT FUCKING TURN!"

On a street in the area of where both Vito and Stranger were killed, Rico and Williams pull up behind Contrares and Vasquez, parked along the sidewalk. Both of these cops are standing outside their car, waiting for the other two to come to them. Rico gets out of the car and stops. He crawls onto the hood of the vehicle. Williams also gets out of the car and stops. He walks around to the front of the car and stands. The other two cops come back to talk.

Williams speaks first. "Well, what the hell happened? Did an old Plymouth outrun you?"

Contrares is noticeably embarrassed. "I don't know. There he was, then there he wasn't." Vasques just looks at his own feet, trying to remain invisible.

Williams continues sarcastically, relishing the opportunity, "Boy, we're really going to have to keep an eye on this Montillo character. He sounds like a pretty tricky driver."

Berman's voice comes in over the radio. "Hey, you guys find each other yet?"

Rico jumps off the car and gets the CC. "We're here Berman. This is Rico."

"You two cars stay together. If you see him again, don't lose him. If you have to take him down on the streets, go for it. We can do the house later, but I think he's got the dope with him."

"O.K. Sarge. We're near the house now. Williams and I will stay close. We'll have Contrares go park it and wait."

Rico makes sure he cuts off mic, gets out of his car and, leaning over the open door talks to others. "Doesn't Montillo live around here somewhere?"

"Yeah, right around the block, on Eighth." All look at Vasquez, the rookie who has spoken for the first time with this vital piece of information.

Rico continues, "Berman wants you guys to park it over there. We'll follow you over there and then we'll stay close, but keep moving.

The asshole is probably heading home." All nod agreement and go to their respective cars.

Williams and Rico are into their car first. While the other two are walking back and out of earshot, Rico asks, "Are you hungry?"

"No," Williams responds without much thought. "I can do without food for a while." He starts the car.

"Well, I'm hungry."

"From the looks of you, hibernation is possible."

Rico doesn't respond.

"Fine. So, let's stop at that little store over there and get you something to eat." Williams points with his head and turns off the car.

"Only one problem."

"What's that?"

"I don't have any money. You wanna lend me five bucks?"

"Shit! Don't you Mexicans ever carry your own money? You'll probably go in there and get involved in a hold-up." Williams reaches into his pocket, as if cracking a safe, carefully taking out a five. "Alright, but hurry up. Contrares is waiting! Freaking JUSTICE is waiting!"

Rico takes money and says, "I actually have money, but I prefer to use yours." As he says this, he dons his red bandana for luck.

Rico opens the door and is just getting out when Vasquez' voice comes in over C.C. *That's him. That's the suspect!"*

Williams looks up and picks up the CC at the same time. "That's him?"

"Yeah, that's the one."

Rico was not fully away from the car and without comment he re-enters, shuts door, and starts to put the five dollar bill into his shirt-pocket, trying not to take Williams' attention. "O.K. Let's take him!"

As Williams begins to follow the suspect, steering with one hand, he holds out the other. Rico reaches into his pocket and takes out the five, but before he can place it into the open palm, the following ensues: Contrares voice breaks the awkward silence. *"We'll come from the other side."*

"I think he's pulling up in front of his place," Williams announces. "We're going to take him!"

Paloma pulls to the side of the road when he realizes that he's being followed. Williams parks directly behind Montillo/Paloma's car and the two cops go into a routine stop procedure. This consists of the driver going up to the suspect's window and the partner going up, behind the suspect, on the passenger's side. Rico starts to un-holster his sidearm, then rethinking it picks up the shotgun and braces it on his hip, pointing slightly downward, in ready position. As he draws his weapon, he also has taken his wallet out, revealing his badge. He stops behind the driver on the passenger side and views Paloma through the rear window. Then Williams arrives at the driver's side window and shows his badge to Paloma who reaches under his seat, slowly, as if he may be going for a gun. This happens to be the place that the dope has been hidden previously, but Rico and Williams don't know this. Rico tenses at the movement and lifts his gun, pointing it at Paloma's head. At the same time Contrares and Vasquez drive up, in the front of Paloma's car, their headlights facing Rico and Williams, but there is one other car between them and Paloma.

Just as Williams is getting to the window, and Rico is just lifting his gun, Contrares and Vasquez are getting out of their car. Contrares and Vasquez's views are momentarily, partially blocked by a van that is between them and Paloma's vehicle.

Contrares approaches from the street, or driver's side and Vasquez jumps to the curb, on the passenger's side. Vasquez is slightly elevated from Rico, as the street is an incline of approximately 20 degrees. Vasquez has never drawn his weapon out of the Academy prior to this moment and already is pointing it in a nervous fashion, as soon as his feet hit the curb.

When Rico comes into view in plainclothes, all Vasquez can see is a shotgun (one that he did not expect) and a man in a bandana (which he had not seen Rico wear). Vasquez immediately opens fire on Rico.

The world slows to a snails pace for Rico and he sees each bullet fly towards him. Although Rico realizes he is being shot, he has not had time to react to what he felt was a non-threat. His weapon remains slightly down and to his side. His badge is the only thing shielding him from Vasquez.

"I'm a cop! It's me. I'm a cop!" Rico hears his own voice as time returns to normal and he falls to the ground. Then he hears a cacophony of voices.

"He's one of us! You don't have to shoot!" Contrares hollers immediately, rushing around the back end of the van, toward Rico, forgetting Paloma completely.

"He's my partner! He's a cop!" Williams also shouts instantly, not wanting to take his eyes off of Paloma.

Vasquez still has his weapon pointed in Rico's direction, and now Contrares' general direction. Williams realizes that he needs to take charge of the situation. "Get out of the fucking car" He thrusts his weapons directly into Paloma's head. Rico can hear other cars approaching and several footsteps.

"You," Williams' voice calls to one of the other officers. "Take this asshole...NOW. And, *you*, get an ambulance!"

There is the sound of footsteps as the other two obey Williams' commands. Rico also hears the sound of handcuffs and of someone running over to him, though his eyes are closed.

Williams quickly moves alongside of Rico's body. Contrares voice can also be heard in the background, on the radio. "Officer shot near the corners of Eighth and West. Officers need assistance. Officers need an ambulance. Officer down."

Rico hears this is repeated one time, and then recognizes Williams voice by his side, "Rico? Rico? Hey Panda?

Rico opens his eyes and speaks feebly, "What the hell do you want?"

Williams relaxes when he realizes that Rico is not dead. "That mother fucker shot our car."

Rico is in pain, but responds, "You asshole."

"It's a good thing that kid couldn't shoot. Where were you hit?"

"I don't know. My stomach. My legs maybe."

Sirens come from every direction.

A woman's voice can be heard over several radios. She is sad, but trying to sound professional. "Officers need assistance. All available units to the corner of Eighth and West. Officer is down. Officer has been...shot."

Rico has to raise his voice to speak over the increasing background sound. "Williams?"

"Yeah?"

"I dropped my gun and my badge. Could you get them for me?"

"Sure."

"And, Williams? I left your five dollars on the car seat."

"I already got it. What do you think I am, stupid? That was the first thing I did. You can't leave money laying around with Mexicans and Jews all around you."

The mixed-voices of several other police officers is heard in the background.

"Who's been shot?"

"Is *he* the one?"

"Did *HE* shoot the cop?"

"Which one? Who the hell is the cop?

"Who shot him?"

"Which ones are cops?"

Rico lifts his face slightly to try and see what's going on. There are a number of uniformed and non-uniformed officers standing, shuffling and hurrying around in all directions. Now, a motorcycle cop breaks through the crowd. Rico watches and sees the big black pair of boots as they stop and then begin a slow steady march directly for him. They look menacing, as if they are going to crush Rico's head. Rico's eyes widen as the boots advance.

Because of Rico's appearance, The motorcycle cop thinks that Rico is the suspect and has shot a cop. Just as the boots get right up to Rico's face, Williams voice comes from behind. "*He's* the cop! He's the cop, you asshole!"

"Well, let's get going then! Get him on my bike. I'll get him to the hospital. Come on, let's get him moving!"

The ever-increasing number of bodies begins to respond to the bike cop's frantic commands, as several officers rush in and pick up Rico. Rico screams in pain as he is roughly and unprofessionally manhandled toward the motorcycle. Suddenly, again Williams' voice takes control as the only one of reason. "There's an ambulance right there!" Without waiting for paramedics, the mosh-pit of officers, changes course and stampedes toward the ambulance.

During the chaos Rico calls out, "My legs! Stop, it's my legs. You're digging your fingers into my wounds."

It is as though no one is listening anymore. Rico hears various comments, from unrecognized voices, *"Where's he shot? Where's the blood coming from?"*

"Get him on the bike!"

"No, put him in the ambulance. The ambulance is here. Put him in the ambulance!"

"Be careful of his legs. I think he's shot in his legs."

After what seems like an eternity, Rico realizes he is being placed into an ambulance. He looks out of the door, seeing all the cops looking in at him, and watches the door being closed as an attendant sits next to him.

The figure of the attendant begins to go out of focus and grow white as it gets blurry. This indicates to Rico that he is passing into a state of semi-consciousness. For an unknown period of time he sees blackness that slowly develops and fades into translucent images of several new figures and then silhouettes.

In Rico's blurry-eyed view he realizes that he is now on an operating table. Everything is unclear visually, but clear audibly. He hears a male doctor's voice say, "The damage to the muscle tissue is too extensive. I doubt he'll ever walk again. I need more suction."

Then, a female voice responds, "Yes doctor."

Then another male voice suggests, "Maybe we should remove the tissue around these fragments."

A different female responds, "Too much chance of infection. Besides the leg would be useless, then, for sure."

The first doctor concludes, "We may as well just amputate in that case."

The second doctor agrees with, "We'd need an O.K. for that."

The female doctor is more cautious, "Let's just put him together the best we can for now. Luckily the gut wound is not serious. That cop was terrible shot. Let's do what we can to save the legs and deal with infection if that happens."

Another doctor completes the thought, "And, if we need to operate again, we can get his release to do what we have to do."

The whole while, Rico can hear every word and wonders, *"How come they didn't give me any anesthetic?"*

When Montillo finally gets through processing, he is literally *thrown* into a large holding cell. He has been *tenderized* during initial questioning and his arms, face and body show signs of rough treatment by virtually every police representative that he came into contact, on his way to lock-up. The holding cell is packed with bodies, coming into the jail system or going out, on their way to release. Ordinarily, every inmate tries not to disturb the delicate balance of power that exists here. In Montillo's case, he is thrown into and on top of many individuals, in the jailer's hope of causing even further disturbance for the guy who "got a cop shot," earlier in the day.

All of the officers' frustrations finally had been funneled away from Vasquez and toward the dealer that was arrested at the scene of Rico's injury. It was almost immaterial that in his truck was found a large amount of high-grade heroin, the largest cache ever made up until that point in L.A. history. What was on ever cop's mind was the fact that Rico Rose had been shot that day, and it was the arrest of Montillo that had been the cause. Montillo allowed the police to put a face on the tragedy.

So, it was particularly disturbing for the cops, when they tossed Montillo into the cell, that he was not beaten further by any of his temporary cellmates. In fact, Montillo's presence had suddenly changed the tense atmosphere in the holding cell. Many inmates actually seemed to focus their attention on cushioning his fall and helping him to a place of honor on the limited sitting space on the wall. News travels faster in jail than anywhere else, and the news of Montillo's arrest and The Panda's demise had already reached within these walls.

"Are you the guy who killed the Panda?" The question came from an elderly, black man who was already seated when Montillo was set gently on the bench beside him.

"I was there when he got shot," Montillo answered cryptically, not sure what *the word* was or how he fit into the jail lore.

The elderly "shot caller" leaned forward, away from the wall where he was leaning to reveal some crude graffiti that had been etched into the wall. There was a panda, wearing a red bandana, crudely etched onto the wall. This picture was new, and significant since there was a particular addition to the pictograph that told a story in graffiti language. The face of the bear had a simple "X" drawn across it. In the language of the streets, this meant that someone who was known as *The Panda* was dead.

Montillo had seen Rico Rose get shot, but he had also seen that the undercover cop was very much alive when he'd been taken from the scene where Montillo had been arrested. Somehow, perhaps through nothing more than the power of wishful thinking, a number of criminals awaiting trials believed that the death of Rico Rose would result in their charges being dropped. Montillo did not want to be the destroyer of hope for his new roommates, especially if it meant destroying his own credibility.

"Yes, I saw him go down," Thinking quickly Montillo added, "I'm not *saying* who shot him, but it happened while they were arresting me."

"So, how would you like us to address you, my friend?" The shot caller wanted to know. For a moment, Montillo thought about using his street-name, *Paloma*, but then realized that it was better to rewrite his own story in case his old mentor still had followers inside who would seek vengeance. "Let's just call me Slayer," he said at last, but while he was answering, a new group of *fish* (inmates) was being cast into the tank. Paloma glanced up to see a half dozen men were stirring up the momentary calm of the cell with their newly infused energies. One new fish's voice was recognized by Paloma, which made his countenance and his demeanor change from one of relative optimism to despair. "If I find the dealer who fed my son the dirty shit, he won't live to see another day. We have a way to deal with child abusers in here." The voice was that of Juanito Carlos' father.

Some time has passed. Rico is in casts up to his hips. There are two casts, so it is clear that Rico did not lose either of his legs. The casts are elevated from pulleys, which are suspended over the bed, from a metal structure. There is a nurse in the room. She is checking his pulse and removing an uneaten plate of food. Rico simply lies there, staring at the ceiling with a despondent look in his eyes. The nurse stops at the door, as if she is going to say something, but remains silent and just shakes her head. There are a number of get-well cards and flowers all over the room, to indicate that Rico is well loved and has been here a while. The door closes slowly and then it is reopened, immediately. Ron is standing outside, peeking in. When he sees that Rico is awake, he enters.

"Hey, Panda. How's the healing coming along?"

"Don't call me that."

"What's eating you? I thought the doctors said that the chance of infection was passed. You may even dance again."

"Big deal. I *might* walk. If I do, I'll be stumbling around for the rest of my life IF I ever get out of a wheelchair. Everything...I ever wanted to be has been taken from me. And for what? Why? To stop some little dope dealer from scoring. Big deal! Did we even get the guy?"

"Sure we got him. We got him with his hands dirty."

"And he was out on the street in less than twelve hours!" Rico looks directly at Ron, and lowers his voice for emphasis. "He was out of jail before I was out of surgery."

"I know it's hard Panda."

"I told you to stop calling me that!"

"Would you prefer I call you Hon?" Ron was trying to be funny.

"No," Rico said remembering the last conversation he'd had with Susie. "But, The Panda? The Panda is dead. He was killed back there when one of the good guys, one of his own fucking guys made mush out of his legs. I'm off the street for keeps, and that's what I lived for."

"Hey, there's more to life than being a cop."

"Like what? Like having someone to love?"

"What're you talking about?"

"Susie's brother, Poncho, called me yesterday and gave me the good news. She's been seeing some other guy for months. The *Panda*. What a joke! So busy putting jerks in jail for poking holes in their arms, idiots that don't give a damn about themselves or their own lives...I can't even keep my own life in order."

Ron grows angry. "God damn it! It was a fluke, a bummer, a hard knock. That's life. Accept it. Or do you want to give up and die because of an accident?"

"That's just it partner. What if it wasn't an accident?"

"What do you mean by that?"

"I've been getting phone calls saying that somebody in our own unit was on the take. The caller says that he was paid to stop the bust and that I got in the way, just like Morelli."

"Come off it, Rose. You got proof of this besides a mysterious asshole on the telephone?"

"I've been kinda laid up. My usual detective skills have been somewhat handicapped." Rico points to his cast.

Ron sloughs off the self-pity and proceeds, "You know how it works on the street. You put a lot of crooks away and sometimes they just don't get over it. I'm sure there are lots of assholes who are glad you're out of the game. But, the kid who shot you was just plain scared. He was a rookie who panicked. There was a time when you would have done the same thing. Got anything else to support the conspiracy theory?"

"There is one other thing. Contrares' and Vasquez' precinct captain came to talk to me a week or so ago. He assured me a full investigation was being conducted. He also told me he had helped get me a full medical discharge. And he reminded me how *dangerous* it would be if I tried to find out anything on my own. That's the word he used, *dangerous*. I don't know what he meant, but I don't trust him. I didn't tell him anything about the phone calls, either. Sometimes I don't know if I'm being paranoid or if there is something really going on that I somehow got mixed up with. I just have a bad gut feeling there are some pretty important people involved in a big cover up, and that's not how it's supposed to be. I feel like I need to get even with someone, but I can't tell the good guys from the bad guys without a damn trial. And even then, you wonder who's paying off the jury and I never made good on my promise to Becky!" Rico begins to drift off, as being bed-ridden has left him very weak.

Ron stays, breathes heavily and is silent a moment, then begins to move slowly toward the door. He stops, turns, begins to speak, changes his mind then decides to make one parting comment. "I don't know what to say about any of this. If someone was paid for a hit, I'll find out. If you want to fight this all the way to the top, I'll do what I can. You were a good cop, one of the best. But you're too good a man to let ANY obstacles stop you, or even slow you down. I gotta go. See you later Panda."

"I just know I gotta do what I think is right." Ron's words have had an effect and Rico speaks as if he's just thought of something, completely on his own. "If I have to fight the entire legal system I will.

The Panda may have died but Rico Rose is still breathing and someday may be kicking." Rico's words fall on an empty room as he drifts off to sleep. *He dreams about being in the Academy. He is being shouted at by the CO. "You're learning to be Police Officers. That makes you special. That makes you different than everyone else, different than you've ever been before. When you get through this training...I mean, IF you get through this training, you're going to know everything that there is to know about surviving. You'll conduct yourselves with precision. Rose?"*

Rico sees the dream as if he is viewing a movie. He sees himself as a young cop. "Yes sir?"

"I want you to do this simulation, and THIS time you won't have to shoot. Is that clear? You won't have to shoot this time."

"Yes sir."

The CO picks out another officer. "You. You'll deal with the driver of the vehicle. Rose, you're back-up."

Rico and the other officer get into position to approach a vehicle. Rico looks confused. This is a re-creation of the approach that took place on Paloma's car. He looks at the other officer. It's Williams. Rico squints his eyes as if trying to remember something. The C.O commands "Do it."

In his dream, young Rico breaks from his pondering and begins to do the approach. All of a sudden, as if it is the night of the shooting, Vasquez, appears from another car, facing them and begins to open fire. Rico looks amazed and scared, holds his badge up in front of himself, like a shield as he yell, "I'm a cop! I'm a cop! I'm a cop!"

Rico awakens hours later to the reality of his hospital room. His eyes are wide open. He inhales a quick gasp, as if he's tasted the breath of life for the first time. He stares at the ceiling of the darkened room. He's covered in sweat and breathing hard, laboring for every lungful of air. Every exhale seems to echo in his brain with the words of his dream, "I'm a cop. I'm a cop. I'm a cop."

Epilogue

Resurrection of the Panda
Or
A Simple Case of Supply and Demand

It was a long and hard recovery for Rico Rose. Permanent damage to both legs made it impossible for him to remain with the department, and he really didn't feel as though he fit in with any other occupation so he floundered for a while. His parents, of course were happy, but his girlfriend had long since given up. Several departments and agencies, organized to fight Rico's medical claim and reduce his retirement, claiming negligence on his part.

It was nothing personal. Saving money, after all is the prime focus of every bureaucratic administration. However, the prime motivator in any man's life is the economic security of his family. Because Rico had met a woman, gotten married and started a family, financial security became his top priority as well. Rico was forced to reengage with the memory of the shooting and to follow-up with the people and the case that lost him the full use of his legs.

He counter-sued not only the officer who shot him, but that officer's superiors, both police departments that were involved, and both the City of San Fernando and the City of Los Angeles—each had been involved in the joint taskforce of which Rico was a part.

Along about 1980, Rico Rose asked his sensei, Johnny Angel (who was a budding freelance writer) to create a document titled, <u>*Death of the Panda,*</u> documenting the incident. Rico got the court to allow him to read that text into the official records, as his testimony for the case. After 10 years, Rico Rose was awarded in the neighborhood of 3.5 million dollars, given full benefits and a full pension.

It's important to remember that the story of Rico Rose, and his abilities as a super-sleuth really did not begin to unfold until *after* his shooting. Because, he seemed always to be operating from a very special place that most of us only dream about, it appeared as if everything he touched simply turned somehow to gold. Where most of us see only defeat, he always saw opportunity.

Let's look at the facts: He was shot five times by someone who had been trained to shoot, but had not been killed. He had been ostracized by the department that he had dedicated his life to, but was rewarded by that same department with a large sum of cash and a full pension. That might have been enough for many of us, but not Rico. He remained friends with all of the people he had once worked with, including those on the many departments to whom he had been loaned.

One day, he saw an ad in the newspaper, looking for a Director of Emergency Services, for the City of San Fernando (his old boss). He applied for the low paying job, and got it. When he showed up for work, most of his staff wondered why he'd want to return to service in this way.

"It's what I do," he told them and got to work doing the best job he possibly could. That meant that he familiarize himself with the requirements of the new position. No one seemed to know what it was that he should be doing, and Rico was given a chance to define his new position himself.

"O.K. Can I take a look at the current Emergency Plan?" He remembered asking on his first day at work.

"That's what you're supposed to be creating," someone had told him.

"We'll do we have any emergency standards and procedures in place?" he asked. "What about an earthquake? Is there any piece of paper that tells us who's in charge or what we're supposed to do during a natural disaster like an earthquake?"

There was no such document. It was obvious to Rico that in earthquake prone, Southern California, that would be a good place to start. So, he took two weeks and concentrated on this single part of the Emergency Plan, detailing what every person's duty would be in case of a severe earthquake. He finished his job on January 14th, 1994. The following Monday, on January 17th, 1994 the devastating Northridge Earthquake struck.

Following his instincts, as usual Rico Rose, the new Director of Emergency Services had made exactly the right choice. He'd concentrated his efforts precisely where they were most needed. When he arrived at Police Headquarters, no one seemed to know what they were supposed to be doing. They didn't even know what Rico had been doing for the first two weeks in his new job. He did not wait for directions. He'd already been told that he was to define the parameters of his new position and he knew that no one else had wanted the responsibility to begin with. Without hesitation, Rico began handing out assignments. "Here, this is a speech that the mayor can deliver," he said, handing a piece of paper he'd drawn up just days before. "And, here are the names of the people in charge of various departments and divisions throughout the city." He had *suggestions* for political leaders, and a press release that outlined the many cooperative efforts that he was about to put into place. In other words, he had defined the role that he was hired for and was now able to demonstrate why his definition was "spot on."

From the moment Rico took charge, it was clear that his Emergency Plan would be effective, even at this level of devastation. Staff and service organizations from neighboring cities and counties allowed the newly appointed Director of Emergency Services of San Fernando to command all resources.

A year after Rico took the job, he returned to the City Council and asked for a raise in salary. His wish was granted, without argument. He moved forward in the project of creating an Emergency Services Handbook that organized all resources and departments, regardless of the emergency, to their best advantage.

He had purchased a home for about $180,000 in San Fernando and then sold it for almost a million dollars more! In that period, Rico was also being called upon to assist in operations for police agencies as a consultant. Naturally, he always helped regardless of the fact that he was not often paid for his services. It just happened to be the thing that he loved to do. Many times, when a state or federal agency was unable or unwilling to assist an individual—though the cause might be a good one—personnel began to suggest that Rico Rose be consulted "outside the purvey of the department."

This often suited Rico better than being an on-duty police officer, since he could never violate any laws when he was just asking questions. He displayed an uncanny ability to ask the right questions, usually uncovering the one piece of evidence or revealing the one flaw in the logical flow that led to the solving of a criminal investigation. Using Rico Rose as a consultant was often referred to as exercising the "Rico Statute," in reference to the legislation which helps to put away career criminals, since results are always more important in the private sector than methods. In addition to his work for the City of San Fernando, he created a very successful private investigation consulting business for himself. He gave up his quest for Morelli's killer because the "word on the street" was that the killer had been somehow punished and, as happens in the underworld, one kingpin was quickly and without ceremony replaced with another.

Later, he trained his sister, Yvette Rose in the ways of investigation and Rico proudly admits, "Yvette is a much better PI than I will ever be."

In addition, Rico learned to limit his handicap and to rely most heavily on his natural instincts to solve problems. He also learned that the greatest lessons in martial arts are those that don't require punching and kicking. What Rico had learned from the martial artist had left a lasting impression on him. The knowledge and discipline helped him tremendously with his physical therapy. Johnny Angel and Rico Rose began to share lessons as John started keeping track of Rico's adventures.

The streets were both of their classrooms and the lessons were endless. As Rico's sensei and friend, John was welcome to follow Rico and had the privilege to learn first hand how he applied his special skills to the new conditions that life had presented. Together, they covered various topics, everything from shooting a firearm to people watching.

One time, Rico and John were on one of these "people watching" adventures when he pointed at some and said, "Look, that guy is on heroin."

Johnny Angel did not believe it and thought Rico had just picked a guy, at random from the crowd and was going to make up an explanation about his background, just to look good.

Rico was adamant though and said, "I'm so certain that he'd on heroin that I'm willing to arrest him, right now just to prove it."

"Arrest him?" John was horrified. They had come to the barrio so that Rico could teach me about what he had done for a living. He wanted to train John in his subtle investigation methods and to let me see him in action so that Mr. Angel could write about it better. Rico Rose had been officially retired from the police force for years and the two had a long history together.

They'd come to this area so Rico could show Johnny Angel how and where he had worked undercover when he was a drug cop. John had not expected to be involved in any arrests, however.

"You can't arrest him. You're retired!" John tried to be logical.

"He doesn't know that," Rico pointed out. All John could do was follow along as Rico stopped the car, jumped out and caught up to the big, burley looking Hispanic who was covered in tattoos. It didn't seem like a good idea to accuse someone of being under the influence, and John expected Trouble (with a capital T) was just a few short words away.

"Hey, hermano. Let me talk to you a moment," Rico said, actually taking hold of the stranger's shoulder and turning him around. It appeared that a fist was about to follow the young man's shoulder, heading straight for Rico's face, but Rico flashed his "retired" police officer's badge, which seemed to block the punch with some magical force. Rico quickly and instantly told the man he was under arrest.

"Oh my God!" John thought to himself. *"This guy does not know the meaning of the word subtle, does he?"*

To his surprise, there was no fight however. The man turned away from the street, toward the wall, as directed, placed his hands outstretched and his legs spread eagle...and assumed the *position.*

"Please stand back, Ma'im," he directed the woman to stand a few feet away and indicated that Johnny, *his sergeant,* would be keeping an eye on things.

"How long ago did you shoot up brother?" Rico got right into the questioning as he wiped his palm along the man's forearms and peered intently as if looking for something.

"I don't know what you're talking about."

John was more worried than ever and his fears became fanciful very quickly. What if this woman had a gun? What if the guy did? What was going to happen when Rico arrested the guy? Were they breaking any laws by showing retired police badges? And, most of all, how did John get to be a sergeant?

"Don't shit me. We don't want to take you in," Rico's tone became friendly. "You're not hurting anyone; I can see that. We just want to ask you a few questions, maybe take your picture or just pictures of your tattoos. As long as you're straight with me, I'll be righteous with you."

"What do you want to take my picture for?" The man seemed to tune right into that statement, almost as much as John had. What was Rico up to?

"It's a new program. We take pictures and keep them on file. If the file keeps coming up with the same photographs...well, that's when The Panda gets pissed."

"What Panda?"

"You never heard about The Panda. You must be new around here."

"This is where my whole family stays vato. But, the Panda is dead."

"If I'm dead...I'm a zombie and that's even worse," Rico's tone was eerie.

"You're the Panda?" The man's affect changed from quiet annoyance to fear. "Hey, man, I heard you was morte. Firme bro'. "

"Let's just say that what you heard was wrong," Rico interrupted. "Now, let's get down to business. How long ago did you pop?'

The man thought only a few moments then responded. "O.K., all right. I had a taste...just a taste, about an hour ago."

Rico glanced imperceptibly in Angel's direction, without any outward expression. John knew he was gloating. It was incredible! He'd been right.

"What about your woman?"

"We're married, man...honest."

"Sure. But, is she flyin' with you?"

"No, man. She doesn't use. She's a good woman! That's mi mijo!"

Just when John thought the whole affair was turning into a family reunion, Rico Rose played his final scene. It seemed as though this last scene was the reason he'd stopped the man in the first place.

"So, you think this is the way you should be bringing up a little kid?"

"No, man. I've tried to stop. I just can't. I'm going to start a new job next week. This was just a taste...one last time, I swear. I'm takin' care of mi familia. "

"Listen, bro' I've been gone for a while and I never met you, but if you've heard about me then you know one thing for reals. The Panda is fair. But, I ain't no chump. I don't want to break up your family, but I don't want *you* to screw it up either. We're going to let you go, but if I see you out here again like this, you're going down, and down hard. Comprende?"

The man shook his head and dropped his arms. He started to walk away, but Rico stopped him. "Hey! Wait! I forgot to take your picture." Rico sent John back to the car to retrieve a Polaroid camera that he had stashed there. John was only gone a minute or two, but while gone, Rico and the other man continued to talk. When John returned he noticed that both the man and woman were now speaking to Rico and, Rico was intent on every word the young couple was saying.

"O.K., I'm ready," John blurted out and pointed the camera awkwardly, snapping one picture randomly.

"Awwww, forget it," Rico said, waving John off, putting his hand over the camera lens as if he were shielding a celebrity from the paparazzi. After shaking hands with the couple, they turned and walked back to the car..

"What was that all about?" John asked, as they were safely out of earshot.

"What do you mean?" Rico asked.

"The whole thing with the camera. You just wanted to get me away from you for a while, so you could talk in private. What didn't you want me to hear?"

Rico smiled out of respect that his sensei and writer had understood his ploy. "It wasn't that I didn't want you to hear, " he said. " I just wanted to give them the chance to talk freely, without the *Sergeant* around. Besides, we can use these photos for our scrape book."

"And, thank you very much for the promotion," John said. " From civilian to sergeant without so much as five minutes in the Academy. What was the topic of conversation, anyway?"

"You mean, what was the real reason I stopped those guys? And, how did I know he had been using?"

"Whatever. Those will be good for starters."

"Well, I can't tell you everything because there's a bust about to happen. What I **can** tell you is that a guy, with no job, shouldn't be that happy and walking around in broad daylight during working hours, with a wife that is also not working and a kid who should be in school."

"He could've been a night watchman or something."

"Night watchmen don't have the same look. That guy was stoned. I recognized that much, even from the car. The tattoos also told me that he was a gang member, or former gang member and probably couldn't *buy* a respectable job, even he he'd wanted one. Finally, it wasn't *him* that I wanted to talk to...it was the kid and the wife."

"The kid and wife? But, you didn't even say a word to the kid."

"When I got close enough to see his eyes, I didn't have to."

"You're not saying that the kid was stoned too, are you?"

"No, but that little boy had the look of a *night watchman*, comprende? That means, *understand*?"

"Not in the least," Johnny admitted, ignoring the insult. Rico went on to explain that a person who has messed up their mind, depending on the drug they are using, has a certain glazed look about them. Some drugs make one's eyes dilate. Other drugs make the pupils smaller, while still others make the cheeks sag or the skill yellow, or the breath stink and so on. If you know drugs and their effects you can actually tell what drug a person is probably using.

"But a person who has been up all night," he went on. "One whose natural clock has been switched around, just looks drawn and tired...just like the little boy. I've been working on something that involves large amounts of something. I think it's heroin. There are lots of people involved. Common junkies, like that man, are getting free drugs...something that he can't afford right now and his woman won't let him go out and rob for it anymore. The boy is in the middle. Mama doesn't want her *chico* to use drugs like the daddy does, but she's a typical street chick with an unshakable loyalty to papa. He keeps telling her that he's going to go straight...something he might even believe at times. And she wants to believe it. In a twisted way, she thinks she can keep the family together, make some money for papa and keep her little one from *using*, by letting him help dad in *the business*."

"What..." John was afraid to ask. "...is *the business*?"

"In this case it's dealing...being The Man...the Dude with the Bag...get it?"

"Not really. Remember, I'm just *training* to be a super sleuth."

Rico laughed as we got back into the car and started the engine of the black Camaro with a roar. A few minutes passed, then he continued. "Lesson one...vocabulary. Dealing is selling drugs. The Man with The Bag, is the guy who sells *Chivas*. That's heroin."

"So the kid is selling heroin?"

"No, it's a mom and pop operation. The boy is the night watchman, like I told you. It's much safer that way. Mom's probably busy during some of the day. Maybe she's even got a real job part-time, but she's also trying to keep dad off of drugs and out of jail, his second home. Dad is also busy, maybe looking for real work some times. But, when you get right down to it, a guy without an education and lots of tattoos can't make as much being honest as he can being bad. There just aren't as many openings. So, he'd a salesman in a market that he understands, trying to sell drugs for the cartels. Those are the real operators, the ones I want to bust. The kids are hired hands, sold-out by their parents for what they believe are noble reasons. I think the kids are the key to the entire operation. The cartels let the dads do some pushing just to get to the kids. Little kids often guard the big stashes and are kind of immune from prosecution. If they get grabbed with a couple hundred thousand dollars worth of chivas, what's going to happen? The judges know that no little kid is a main Man. The kids walk."

"So, where does that leave us right now?"

"We're on our way to the ghetto to check out another part of my theory. Any questions?"

"Just two. What theory? And, aren't we already in the ghetto?"

***

A few miles later, John was still confused, and, Rico did not help the matter by performing another unexpected act. He pulled into a low income, Housing Project's courtyard, with about a dozen gang members huddled around a short stone wall, and leaped out of the car with his badge waving. "Everybody stay still. We just want to talk."

Incredibly, no one moved. "Lieutenant, if you don't mind, I'll handle this," he said. John supposed he was talking to him, so he stayed back, near the car. John, therefore didn't hear much of what was being said, but if he had, it wouldn't have done me much good since every word was in Spanish. The conversation was short and to the point, but John had a enough time to survey the situation. "What a perfect place to be shot by a sniper," John thought to himself. They were in a man-made box canyon of sorts. Dozens of windows surrounded us on each of four sides. We would never even have known where the shot had come from.

Just then, before John could get too worried, one of the little guys took a swing at Rico. Until that moment, the guy hadn't made a single move. In fact, he hadn't appeared to be that interested in Rico at all. John was totally taken unawares by his action, and prepared for an all out fight, trying to decide if he should jump back in the car and run over a few or leap into the fray to help out. Johnny did not have to make a single move, however.

Of course, Rico had told me that he'd trained in the martial arts for many years. But he is not a tall man, and he'd also been shot five times in his legs, so John expected very little help from him when it came to punching and kicking. John was wrong in that assumption, mainly because he did not know that Rico had been practicing new, modified techniques to compensate for his disabilities ever since the shooting. He had learned to use his body-weight and low center of gravity to their best effectiveness. He had also been training in the Filipino art of Kali or short stick fighting, as used a cane on many occasions.

So, John was surprised to see that before the first blow even struck, Rico had moved **directly toward it** with his whole body. At the same instant, both hands came to a ready position, in front of his head and chest and were simultaneously thrust forward. The result was a triple-score. The attacker's blow was cut short and struck the top of Rico's head before the other guy was ready for it. He actually hurt his wrist on top of Rico's head. The second hand immediately hit the little guy in the face, while the chest-high hand (which was in a flat palm position) pushed forward in a double thrusting motion and actually seemed to hit its target twice. The kid, a young teen, went down of his own momentum, holding his wrist, his nose and gasping for breath. It was a truly Bear-Like maneuver.

Now John really expected trouble, anticipating the rest of the gang to jump us immediately, but there was only a quiet lull. In the interruption, John was hoping to seize the opportunity for escape, but another of Rico's action took me again by surprise.

He pulled a $100 bill out of his shirt pocket and tried to hand it to one of the young men who, he later told me, appeared to him, to be in charge. But, instead of grabbing it up, the gang member waved it off and shook his head, completely uninterested. Rico offered it one more time, to another, younger boy wearing a baseball cap, but was again refused.

He held the bill for all to see, said a few words, shrugged and put the hundred back in his pocket. The whole incident seemed like a pretty lame stunt to me...until, of course, Rico got back into the car and explained his actions. He has a way of making the craziest stunts seem perfectly logical.

"We could've been killed!" John growled through his teeth when we were happily out of danger and on the road once again. "I'm not sure I can survive the training process necessary to even write about somebody as crazy as you."

"Why are you so exaggerated? Nobody even frowned in your direction...Lieutenant."

John couldn't help but laugh at that. Maybe my life was being put, unnecessarily in constant danger by hanging around with this guy, but at least I *was* getting regular promotions in rank.

"O.K., O.K! But, will you at least tell me what that whole thing was about?"

"Just checking a hunch and a lead."

"What's that supposed to mean?"

"That's what good detective work is based on," Rico clarified with a grin. "Sure, some of it is hard work, but you gotta check your leads and have faith in your hunches and then there's one more thing. Probably the one thing that separates the very best from the average investigator."

"O.K. professor, give it to me in one small bite so I don't choke," John knew he was about to be insulted, may be in a subtle way, but an insult no less. The beauty of Rico's charm is that while he'd making fun of you, you really don't care.

"First, before I tell you that, let me say that we have a long night ahead of us. You don't have any plans do you?"

"Tonight? Saturday, for a married man with a nervous wife? No, fine I'm all yours."

"Bueno!...That means *good* in Spanish, and I think you should try and learn some Espanol if you're going to be hanging around with me."

"I should also buy a bullet proof vest," John added. "But, Spanish lessons aren't what you had in mind for tonight's entertainment, is it?"

"No, tonight we're going to stake-out a warehouse. It 's becoming obvious that something I've been working on and what I've learned tonight from our home boys and that kid and his mom are connected. There are a lot of drugs floating around for free. I found that out when I offered $100 for $10 worth of the stuff. Usually those junkies would have jumped on that money. But, none of them even seemed interested. That means that they, like the guy we stopped earlier, are too satisfied. They must be getting *free samples* or they're taking advances on stuff that's about to hit the common market. I think I know where some of the stuff is coming from, but I'll explain all that later during our long night together."

"So, is that it? Is staking out the third thing that a great detective has to know about?"

"No, staking out is usually a waste, although important at times. Mainly we'll just sit in a car, drink coffee and pee in alleys. It's the part of detective work that few people talk about."

"So, then?" John tried to coax it out of him, but was forced to ask the question. "So, besides following up on leads and hunches, what is the other thing that makes detectives great?"

"You have to be basically a builder of ideas. You have to be suspicious and want to fill in the spaces. In other words, the final thing is that you first need to *have* hunches to follow up on. "

***

Without so much as a goodbye, Rico dropped me off at my house, saying only that he'd pick me up again at around midnight. That would be two hours later. A shiver ran through my entire body and it was not due to any unknown mystery. It was the result of what I knew for a fact to be true. I'd driven through the barrio for hours and actually *looked* for trouble, making myself a small white target in a neighborhood that John truly did not belong in. Now, John was going to sleep in a car with a guy that I barely understood. It wasn't easy to explain to his wife.

John cleaned up, packed a few things and Rico was right on time. At the door, John was stopped cold by taking a quick glance at the difference in Rico's and my mode of dress.

He was "made for the street" with blue beanie, dark glasses (even though it was midnight), baggie jeans and a red and white Pendleton. John was a bit more GQ. When John realized his mistake, John tried to *slouch* by way of fitting in better. Rico just giggled and when we got to the car, John gladly accepted a leather jacket to complete his disguise.

John had been so self-conscious about my clothing that he did not notice the car that was following us, and which had been parked outside my door, across the street and down a few houses until Rico pointed it out to me.

"You know we're being followed?" he asked when we were finally moving.

"No," John turned around and saw the car glued to our tailpipe as Rico sped up quickly and made a series of sharp lefts and rights.

"...I mean, of course I knew it," John changed my story, so as not to appear too much the dork.

"Was everything *normal* at your place? Did you see any *other* cars parked outside?" He was trying to sound casual, but I'd been around him enough by then to realize that he seldom made small talk; therefore he probably was concerned.

"I didn't see any cars," John said. Then, he realized how serious the situation had become. "Could I be in some kind of danger? What about my wife?"

Rico's actions answered his questions pointedly, John thought. Rico's foot came down on the accelerator with such a force that the floorboard shook, and the engine responded the way it was supposed to, pressing me back against the seat and forcing the blood into my ears. He turned quickly, suddenly changing directions, 180 degrees.

The car that had been following us must have wondered what the hell was happening. They literally stopped in the middle of the road as we skidded circles around them and raced back in the direction that we came from.

John watched them over my shoulder. They were so confused by Rico's actions that they finally turned around, and then stopped again. When Rico and Johnny were almost out of sight, John saw them turn once more and drive away.

By the time John was getting ready to ask who they were, we had arrived back at my house.

"Nope, nobody here," Rico said casually, and started driving back the way we had headed originally.

"But, what about those guys we just ditched? Who else are we expecting? Aren't they the bad guys?" John wanted to know.

"No, those guys were cops!"

Now, John was riveted, waiting for an explanation. His confusion was dependent on two points. John wanted to know why they were running away from the police, and who else Rico had come back to check for.

"I thought you realized," Rico began in a friendly, but condescending manner. "Those guys were cops."

"Cops?"

"Yes. They're just looking for an easy score. I do all the work, and they jump in at the last minute and take all the credit. Actually, those are the guys who hired me. I was just having some fun with them. The fact that I was concerned about you, is, because cops aren't the only ones who follow people. In fact, druggies and other assorted bad people have a habit of following *cops* around. The philosophy is that if everybody is watching everybody else, then nobody can get an advantage, see?"

"So you thought that, since those guys had followed me..."

"...Then someone might have been following THEN. Don't get paranoid," Rico cut me off. "Those guys were following *me*. When I dropped you off, they probably just took a lunch break. When I came back to pick you up, I saw them still sitting there. I was just concerned that somebody else didn't end up at your house...by accident...or by seeing those two jokers out in front of your place. Nobody there. Nothing to worry about. And, since it turns out that everything is fine. This just goes to prove my original theory."

"Which is?"

"The bad guys are too relaxed and too comfortable. That makes me *really* scared. They don't think that they NEED to keep an eye on anyone. It follows that whatever it is they are up to is *in place*. I think, this little talk has put it all together for me. In fact, we can solve the whole matter right now, I think, by following up on a simple tip. Do you still want to come along?"

Reluctantly, John's writer's instincts got the better of him and he decided to "go out and play" a little longer. Rico assured John that his wife was in no danger and that he would keep his sensei safe, and merely wanted to satisfy his own curiosity with the solving of a mystery...first hand. They both knew that following a story to the end was a passion that neither could control. It was the main reason that John hung around with Rico in the first place. The "professional relationship" was merely a convenient excuse.

They drove about fifteen minutes at high speed on the Valley freeways. It's hard to determine how far they traveled, because Rico always drove much faster than John ever did. "It's a privilege, " he explained, " ...of carrying a badge. It would be a shame not to use that privilege, especially when it's so much fun."

"So, cops and former cops never get tickets?"

"Of course they do! There are assholes out there who'll give anyone a ticket. But, the odds are low. And, remember, this is **my** territory. I probably worked with these guys somewhere along the line, when I was still wearing blue."

Suddenly, upon leaving the freeway, Rico's style of driving changed radically. He slowed to a nerve-wracking crawl, rolled down the windows and the car and blasted the radio. They were in the barrios, his homeland. He knew that to avoid attracting attention, he had to alter the way he was driving. Only stupid cops or "to the curb" addicts were in a hurry around here.

At a certain point, John found himself *Low-rider cruising* into an alley in an industrial area. The two men parked the car and Rico surveyed the area, slowly and carefully to make sure that they were not seen, or, at least that no one had paid undo attention to their arrival.

"So, what are we going to do now?" John asked, after what he felt was a polite interval.

"This is the unmentioned part of detective work," Rico said. "This is the reason that many people don't go into this work, in fact."

"Danger?"

"No, boredom. We just have to sit here until something happens."

"What are we waiting for? I mean, should I at least be looking at a particular building?" John asked.

"Not yet. For now, just watch **all** of them." John could tell that Rico was looking at him out of the corner of his eye and laughing, although he made no physical movement in John's direction.

The two just sat and watched the loading docks and back doors of several warehouses and industrial buildings. Some doors were open, other closed. People moved in and out, or within a building, all seemingly performing ordinary, warehouse-like functions.

They sat for hours as trucks came and went, loading and unloading, picking up and delivering. All the people looked ordinary and about average to John, but, as time went on, Rico's attention became more and more pinned on one particular building.

John could see Rico was concentrating on his left side, just in front of the car and focused his attentions there too. John could still see no particular reason why though.

Mostly, there was no activity at all. Was there something about the way the men dressed who unloaded the few boxes that come in? None that John could see. He became obsessed with figuring out what set this group apart from the rest. Was it the timing? Were the trucks coming and going with any pattern? No, that wasn't it. From what John could see, all the trucks moved at about the same pace. Just before a truck arrived, the dock-bay doors would open and men would come out. There were four or five men working together on each vehicle and when the truck they were working on was empty, it drove away and they closed the doors. Were the people moving inside in a suspicious manner? That was not it either. Some men seemed lazier or more awake then others, but they were just regular men. None seemed high on drugs, or drunk or even particularly worried. Finally, John could stand it no longer and had to ask another question.

"O.K., I give up! What's so special about that warehouse?"

Rico looked at him, directly, with a mixed expression of disbelief at my dumbness and amusement at my agitation. "Sensei, don't you notice anything different about that warehouse?" He asked, at last, seeming to really want to know.

John looked again to be certain, and then shook his head with confidence. "Not a damn thing is different."

"You've been watching the other operations, haven't you? And, still you don't see anything different. Well, don't feel bad. The police have been out here, at my request, and they haven't noticed anything unusual either. But, that's what makes me such a good detective. A good detective looks at the facts, analyzes them. He doesn't judge at first. He just gets as much information as he needs to form a hypothesis. Getting as much information as possible is ALWAYS a good idea, no matter what you are trying to accomplish. You taught me that."

He winked at John and added, "That's what we police types sometimes call a *hunch*. When we get a hunch, we see if the facts fit. If they do, then we have a theory, and we gather more facts until we can either prove or disprove what we believe."

"Thanks for the lesson," John said, trying to be civil. "And, now, what's the bottom line? Why are we watching that warehouse instead of the others?"

"The bottom line, of course, is always the most important thing," Rico admitted. "All that other shit is worthless if you haven't got one other element."

"What other element, is this?"

"First, let me ask you to re-examine the facts. Close your eyes and tell me what you *know* about warehouses from what you've seen tonight?" He sounded like Sergeant Friday, and he knew it, but John played along.

After all, John was a writer and he had been taking notes. When John was finished Rico gave him a hearty, "Hmmmnnn" of approval and then spoke, "Well, that's too bad," he said somewhat sadly. "After all that observation…and notes…you've missed the point completely."

Rico tried to imitate John's voice, when he was giving him a martial arts lesson.

"And what IS the point?" John nearly yelled, also completely missing Rico's imitation.

"All these places have trucks coming and going right?"

"Right."

"All have similar kinds and numbers of people?"

"Yes."

"No one catches our attention with their behavior?"

"No, No One!"

"But, how much stuff have you seen *go out* of this place?" he pointed to the building in question, and the obvious hit me like a ton of warehouse boxes.

NO merchandise had come *OUT* of that building.

"It's kind of an interesting business that just *buys* stuff, wouldn't you say?" His question made me feel kind of small at first, then angry.

"That's it? Nothing else?"

"Well, I guess it's also unusual that the dock-workers are opening the door right BEFORE anyone shows up and closing right after. My guess is that the truck driver calls when he's around the corner to make sure that it's safe. The boys open the doors, transfer the goods and then go back to watching T.V."

"How do you *know* any of this? What makes you think that this is unusual?" John argued, simply for the sake of saving face.

"That's that final element I told you about," Rico said coyly. "I had *inside information.* Someone TOLD me that something strange was going on here."

Well, this just didn't seem fair to John. *"He made me play along with this, so called, lesson and he already knew which building we were supposed to watch!"* John thought to himself then said aloud, "You knew all the time? How?"

"Well, I didn't know exactly which building, " he said. Answering in a way that some how made John feel better, yet more confused. "I had heard from several people who give me information that strange things were going on in this area. And, either because they didn't know for sure, or didn't want to tell ALL they knew, I was only slowly led to this alley. I was pretty sure that we'd see something, so I brought you along tonight. Don't feel bad," he said in a consolatory tone. "If you knew what we were looking for you would have gotten it right?"

Rico also explained that he'd gone back into the neighborhood to visit with the youngster, mother and father we'd stopped on our night of joy riding. He'd seen both the father and the boy hand small folded bits of paper to several people and not receive any money in return. This, along with other information he'd gathered from snitches, weaved together the tale in its total complexity.

The father had used the boy as a guard of the stash in the early stages. This was a common practice. If the police had rushed the operation, before it could have been fully established, the only person they would have found would have been the boy. Since he was young, he wouldn't have received any punishment. Later, when the father felt secure, he had replaced his son in his guard duties. Apparently, the father had been hired to oversee the operation because of his family ties. Whoever was in charge wanted men and women who could be trusted. That trust was assured to a certain degree if wives and children were placed in jeopardy. The real *businessmen* in the operation, the men removed from the handling of the drugs but who were in charge and would benefit in the end from the sales, would have thought nothing of killing wives and children if their overseers had messed up. At the time that was deemed optimum, all the stash would be released to the dealers. The market would be flooded and everyone would already be *wanting* the drugs, due to the free samples. Hence the value of advertising.

After hearing Rico's explanation, John realized that he had done the best he could do with just a little training. Some people were simply better at detecting than others. Luckily, John was better at both fighting and writing than Rico. He told Rico how much he admired his ability.

"Then you won't mind if I point out one more piece of information to you, something that I just learned tonight?"

"Go for it," John told him boldly.

"There's something else that's different about this warehouse." They looked back as another truck had pulled in and was being unloaded. Rico narrated, as they watched. "If you look at the other warehouses, you see how easily some boxes are lifted and how heavy others are? But, at OUR warehouse, all the boxes are the same...and none of them is heavy, even though they are fairly large. Doesn't that make you wonder WHAT it is that's in those boxes?"

"They're big boxes," John offered, sheepishly.

"They're also mostly empty," Rico said. For some reason, that statement was completely unexpected.

"Huh?" was all the retort John could muster.

"Well, they're not ALL empty, but most of them are, I'd guess. And, the ones that ARE filled may only have a few kilos?"

"Heroin?"

"No, that was the thing that showed me that I'm getting out of touch with the modern day."

"What do you mean?" John asked, noticing a sincere sadness in his tone.

"I found out that heroin is yesterday's high. These guys are dealing something new, probably cocaine, in various forms."

Rico had been in a duel battle for the past five years. One battle was waged to rehabilitate his body from effects of five gunshot wounds. The other battle was a mental one, for he was forced to quit the work that he loved and that he did so well and to face the fact that all cops were not necessarily as good as he was at figuring things out.

A lot had changed in the time he'd been away from the streets. Cocaine, Crack, Ice, Crystal Methedrine, these popular drugs were merely playthings for the rich in the time of Rico's shooting but now everybody was in the game. In a way, he had a lot to learn.

"So, what do we do now?" John asked, believing that they were going to rush in and make the arrests, just the way it was done on T.V.

"Nothing of course. We're investigators, not tag-team wrestlers. I don't want to get into Fist City with a bunch of dockworkers. I already took one punch to the head tonight." Rico was firm but controlled.

This was police business and, it became obvious, the less his face was seen the better he'd be able to do the job that he did so well. Rico started the car and drove slowly out of the area, radio blaring the entire time.

When they were in a neutral neighborhood, Rico stopped and called a number that he had written on a scrap of paper and pinned to his dash-board.

It was only 2:00 A.M., and by 2:15 A.M the car that had followed them earlier drove up and two men got out. Rico greeted the driver and his passenger with smiles and handshakes and both wrote feverishly in tiny note pads while Rico spoke, appearing to lecture. John assumed he was giving them the details of the case. While he spoke, another car, an unmarked one with a couple of other characters dressed in cartoon-gray suits showed up and joined the party. Handshakes all around again and Rico returned to the car. All four of the other men, turned in John's direction and waved before leaving.

"So, who were those guys? Old friends?" John asked, immediately upon Rico's return to the car.

"Well, I knew one of them. Good guy, hard worker. The first two were cops for L.A. and the other two...the ones who dress sort of like you do...were D.E.A., that's *Drug Enforcement Agency*. They'll take it from here," Rico added, rather sadly.

"Do you get anything out of this?" John was indignant. "They're going to take all the credit, don't you at least get some money?"

"Of course I do! It's a hobby, but I gotta eat!"

So, John was satisfied that Rico was satisfied and realized that this was even better for Rico than being a police officer. Rico has the ability to be totally into a case and then, forget about it the next day, after it is solved. The solving of the mystery was everything to him.

For John, it was enough to be there first hand and to see on the news a few days after a report of the *"Largest Cocaine Seizure in U.S. History!"* The name of Rico Rose was not mentioned.

Johnny Angel had been there when The Panda had come back from the dead, and regained his rightful place as the underground champion of right for right-sake. The incredible part of the story is...it was only the beginning. John could still hear Rico's voice telling his teenaged children about his days in the department, always beginning each tale with the same words, "I can't tell you everything, but there I was in the face of danger."